A Bluestocking for the Rake

Spinsters and Rebels

Samantha Holt

Helstone Press

Contents

Chapter One

Ginny never thought she'd miss long gowns.

She'd been wrong.

Now she practically hungered for the caress of flowing fabric that swirled about her legs unhindered.

Once, when she'd suffered the embarrassment of accidentally shutting her skirts in a door. The ominous rip meant a miserable trip to the modiste who spent much of the visit tutting over her unfeminine figure and debating whether any color possibly suited her plain features.

She smoothed her hands down the tabby wool trousers and wrinkled her nose. Her mother would hardly believe she was pondering the virtues of an elegant gown.

The slam of a hand on the kitchen door snapped her attention to the hiss of steam from the kettle.

"Is my cuppa ready yet, boy?" called a customer through the closed door.

Ginny rolled her eyes. The majority of customers visiting her sister's inn were polite and grateful for a break from their arduous journey. Another issue with being disguised as a boy, however, was the few rude ones that felt quite at ease treating her as though she was barely worth waving a hand at.

She grabbed a cloth and used it to lift the hefty kettle with a grunt. Loose shirt sleeves hindered her view as she carefully poured the boiling water into the teapot with a frown on her face. A soft sigh of exasperation escaped her nostrils.

How could she be so wrong about men's clothing? She could

count on her hand the number of times she'd been wrong about anything.

Perhaps she was wrong about running too. Wrong about disguising herself, wrong about hiding in this tiny village.

Ginny almost wished she was still in London, and that she could be at the modiste's again, standing motionless while the woman scolded her for lacking poise, all the while her mouth remaining clamped around pins that would likely end up jabbed into Ginny's skin.

Being treated as though she were nothing more than a combination of her body parts felt almost better than trying to work in uncomfortable clothes whilst keeping her long hair tucked under an itchy hat.

Carefully arranging teacups on a tray, she forced herself to ignore another slam to the door and a repeated demand for her to hurry.

She blamed her mother. Mother's desire to scale the heady rungs on London society meant Ginny had worn only the most precious of fabrics in recent years. One would think wearing breeches would be a welcome relief from the constrictions of fashionable gowns but not when one's breeches were made from the itchiest fabric and seemed to constrict one's, well, private area.

She battled the impulse to wrench the close-fitting trousers away from her legs and tug at the bindings constraining her chest.

Not necessary, dear, Mother would probably say.

But it was entirely necessary.

Ginny might not be endowed with much but whatever happened she could not be discovered.

Her fiancé could never know she was hiding in Oakfield, and he most certainly could not know she was currently disguised as a boy.

Ginny ran a finger along a collar that insisted on strangling her with a sigh. Give her a silk gown with pointless buttons and gossamer lace that caught on pointy ferns any day.

Still, with any luck, Sir Horace Robertson wouldn't even bother searching for her. That pompous, self-important excuse for a man could find plenty of women who would gladly become the obedient wife he wanted.

The funny thing was, she'd been willing to be obedient. She'd hoped to be a helpmate, to aid him in all his research so long as it meant she could be involved. But he made it clear he wanted more than that.

Far more than that.

"You would be a lot more comfortable in a dress."

Ginny yanked her finger from the collar and met her sister's narrowed gaze.

The peaceful atmosphere of the inn kitchen was suddenly disrupted by the sound of people talking and laughing, accompanied by the jingling of forks and knives, and the clanging of tankards being placed on tables.

Maisie deposited a stack of dishes next to the basin. Her face rosy and her hair slightly disheveled, Ginny's sister rushed around the kitchen in an orderly fashion, cleaning up the mess left behind by Ginny as she served breakfast to their visitors.

She'd have to try harder to be tidier. The last thing she wanted to do was make more work for Maisie, but messiness seemed to be somewhat in her nature.

Her sister wiped her hands on the cloth hanging from her apron pocket and folded her arms while she studied Ginny. "Do you not think you are taking this running away and remaining in disguise thing a little too far?"

"I thought it through very carefully."

A lie really, but no one would suspect Ginny of having jumped rashly into this mess, least of all her eldest sister. For someone who carefully planned out every hour of her day, this whole disguise business was quite out of character.

As was stealing Sir Horace's carriage.

Oh yes, and lying to her sister about it.

Should she add fibbing to her family of her whereabouts in a brief letter to them to her list of lies too?

There was no denying it. This whole escapade left her feeling as though being disguised as a boy was the least odd thing she had ever done at this point.

"I cannot believe no one has recognized you yet."

Ginny resisted an unladylike snort. Maisie was all redheaded and curvaceous—someone people noticed. Half the time, no one knew little Genevieve Beaufort even existed. The last thing anyone expected was for her to be dressed as a boy and working at the inn her sister ran.

"Do not forget that half the residents of Oakfield are ancient, and the other half are new and have little idea of the history of the Beauforts here."

Anyway, her disguise was most excellent, even if she had not particularly thought it through, nor really considered the logic behind running away and pretending to be a boy.

"Do not underestimate them," her sister warned her as she undid her white apron then hung it on an iron hook near the door. "Before long, someone will figure out who you are."

"And by then, Sir Horace will have chosen another bride, and I shall be free."

"You could still be free."

Ginny shook her head. Perhaps. Reason told her that Sir Horace would track down his stolen carriage in nearby Hambleton then return to London and console himself with another bride who would be the meek, biddable wife he wanted.

But logic had nothing to do with how she felt about the man she'd met all but once.

A shudder travelled down her spine when she recalled the sensation of his thin lips pressed hard against hers. He didn't just want biddable, though. He wanted a prisoner.

Reason had fled after that forced embrace. Logic left her feeling desperate. The only thing she could rely on was instinct and that told her to get as far away from Sir Horace and his slimy kisses as she could and stay hidden until she knew the waters were safe.

"It's best that I stay here." She met her sister's concerned gaze. "That is, if you do not mind."

Maisie tilted her chin and regarded her with a tender expression that made her vaguely uncomfortable.

"Oh Ginny, you're my little sister. Of course I do not mind, though you know you do not need to work for me."

"I cannot take advantage, Maisie." She rubbed the end of her nose as it tingled. She knew she could rely on Maisie. She was the only one who ever went against their family and understood what it was like to want something other than a staid life in London.

Her sister laughed. "In case you have forgotten I am engaged to a viscount. I do not think it's possible for you to take advantage."

"It's about time you two courted."

Maisie waved her hand in Ginny's direction, a rosy shade of pink bubbling up on her cheeks. Ginny was glad that her sister was so passionate about the wedding and so deeply and truly in love with Apollo. For two reasons really. Her sister deserved happiness with a man she had loved for what felt like Ginny's whole life, but it also meant fewer questions about why she fled from Sir Horace or what she planned to do next.

"I only hope everyone does not fret when they realize you are not really visiting with friends in Bath."

"It will take them a while to figure that one out. I sent my letter via a correspondent in Bath."

"One day you will not have an answer to everything, Ginny," Maisie warned.

Ginny blinked.

Perhaps her sister was right. Perhaps she didn't have an answer for everything. But she had to keep up the facade of control, at least until she figured out her next move. Maisie didn't know the whole truth behind her escape, and she couldn't bear to tell her. It was better to keep it a secret, to avoid any further complications.

"I'll be fine," Ginny said, forcing a smile. "I'm just grateful you're letting me stay here."

Maisie smiled back, her eyes softening. "I'll always be here for you, Ginny, no matter what."

Ginny felt a lump form in her throat, and she swallowed hard, trying to fight it back. She couldn't bear to show any weakness, not in front of her sister.

"Thank you," Ginny said softly. "I'll make sure to repay you for everything."

Maisie waved her off. "Don't be silly, Ginny. You don't owe me anything. Just get that wretched man his cup of tea and I'll be back from Apollo's as swiftly as I can."

"Now that I can do," Ginny assured her sister.

∞∞∞

"So, it's my thirteenth birthday, right?"

Youssef glanced around the inn and motioned to the young lad scurrying about the inn serving ale with a sigh. "I think I'll need another drink if this is going to be one of your long tales."

The inn was a modest-looking place, clean with low beams, and sturdy furniture. The clatter of mugs, the creak of a chair as someone shifted their weight, and the soft hum of chatter from the bar provided a pleasant hum of sound that enabled Pierce and Youssef to converse in privacy from their corner table.

None of the pleasantness meant Pierce liked this damned place any more than any other coaching inn.

"You asked why I hate taverns," Pierce pointed out.

Youssef ran his fingers over a thick dark beard and propped his face on his hand. "And I'm already regretting it."

"So, it's—"

"Your thirteenth birthday, I know." Youssef traced a finger over a scratch in the wooden table.

They'd been lucky to find a seat in the crowded tavern. The last time Pierce had been home, the inn had been closed and Oakfield was home to a handful of slow, elderly people. A lot had changed in two years.

Pierce tightened his gaze on his friend. Youssef's lips quirked and he motioned for Pierce to continue.

"Anyway, my great uncle Colin decides it's time for me to become a man."

Youssef straightened. "He didn't take you to a damned brothel—"

"Lord no. He brought me to an inn much like this one."

Relaxing, Youssef propped his face back up on his hand. "Ah."

"He decides, in his great wisdom, that weak ale is not good enough for a young lord-to-be. I need to experience the strong stuff."

"Liquor?"

"Indeed."

Youssef smirked. "Thirteen and drinking liquor. Why do I fear this isn't going to go well?"

For many boys, the night might have ended up with their head in a bucket. Pierce wasn't that lucky.

"Under my uncle's watchful eye, I forced down two glasses of whiskey."

"Good Lord."

"Everyone is cheering me on, praising me for being a hardy lad..."

"So far, so good."

"The next thing I know, I wake up with a mouth like sand, I've a pounding headache, having passed out at the table, and it's completely dark."

"The whiskey knocked you senseless."

Pierce rubbed the back of his neck and rolled his shoulders. "I swear my neck cracks because of having spent an entire night with my cheek pressed to the bloody table."

"Doubtful, but do go on."

He took a deep breath. He'd faced any number of dangers and pitch-dark nights. He'd endured harrowing crossings where he swore the ship would sink beneath him and camped in deserts while the wind and sand swirled about him and threatened to tear his tent from its pegs. Yet none of those moments made his stomach feel as though he'd swallowed a ton of stone.

Unlike every time he stepped foot in a bloody inn.

"As I said, the inn is completely dark. No one around. No sign of great Uncle Colin."

Youssef chuckled.

"I try to be brave but I'm thirteen if you recall."

"I do."

"I call for Uncle Colin and no one responds. It's practically black—I can barely find my way around the inn—and, bear in mind, this place was a good five miles from home, and I'd never been there before."

Youssef scowled and scanned the room. "Where is that boy? I'll definitely need another ale after this story."

Pierce ignored his friend. "I'm clambering about the inn, probably still drunk, bawling my eyes out. The sort of ugly crying that leaves you all red and runny nosed when you're a boy."

"Speak for yourself. I never cried."

"Liar. You cried on that crossing to Mexico."

Youssef motioned with his finger and thumb close together. "We were an inch from death on that crossing."

"By the time I find the front door, I'm a mess. Just a sobbing, ugly mess of a boy."

Youssef snorted. "Some fine lord-to-be you were."

"I go to open the door and…boo! Someone jumps out of the dark at me, a lantern in hand."

"Your uncle?"

Pierce nodded. "I'm so terrified and worked up at this point, I drop straight to the ground and black out for a moment. When I come to, I'm surrounded by the patrons of the pub, all laughing and toasting me on my birthday. The bloody bastards had doused all the lights and snuck out as soon as I fell asleep."

"Some birthday," Youssef muttered through quirking lips.

Pierce shook his head. He scarcely remembered his other birthdays, despite his parents relishing such occasions with cake and even a few presents.

"With a trembling voice, I ask my uncle why he would do such a thing and he crouches low, puts a hand to my shoulder and tells me 'Well, my boy, it's your birthday.' He then grins—the biggest grin I've ever seen, just pure delight in his eyes and adds, 'and no birthday is complete without a birthday surprise.'"

"Christ. And you liked this man?" Youssef scoffed, though there was an obvious hint of admiration in his eyes.

Pierce shrugged as he recalled the moment in vivid detail, even after all the years that had passed since that night at the inn.

"Uncle Colin showed me things that I didn't know existed and places I never imagined. He taught me how to talk without fear and gave me the confidence to stand up for myself. He showed me there are more ways of being a man than just fighting or drinking."

"Doesn't sound like it with that story."

"Unfortunately, the man also loved a good prank."

And while Pierce gained his love of travel and adventure from his uncle, he'd never understood how the man took so much pleasure in a jape.

Youssef shook his head, then motioned impatiently to someone behind Pierce. "And the point of that story was...?"

Pierce shrugged. "You asked why I hate pubs."

"It's a fine job we're staying with your family then and not here." He scowled. "With how long this damned boy is taking to bring me another ale, I'm beginning to hate them too."

Following Youssef's gaze, he watched the boy nearly spill a tray of drinks, his face flashing a deep shade of red as he mumbled something and kept his gaze to the floor.

"There's something strange about that boy," Pierce muttered. He'd noticed the lad as soon as they entered the bustling building, but he couldn't figure out what it was that had caught his notice about a young man so plain in appearance.

"You know, sometimes, things are just what they seem. Not everything is a mystery to be unraveled."

Admittedly, Pierce had a tendency to look for mystery everywhere. He blamed Great Uncle Colin for that too. Growing up on tales of adventures had left Pierce with the itching desire to follow in his uncle's footsteps. Anything seemed better than sitting around waiting for his father to die so he could be the next Duke of Marbury. There were many men who couldn't wait for the moment they pried the title from their father's clutch.

Pierce was not one of them. He hoped his father lived a long, happy life.

"Well, we still have this mystery to decipher." Pierce jabbed a finger at the creased, torn, and stained piece of paper that had lived upon his uncle's person apparently. "We need to figure out what this bloody map means."

"I think it's the stone circle at Crosland. Those lines look like little stones to me."

Pierce leaned in. The sketch was so old and crude it could be almost anything but, if the map had almost been buried with Great Uncle Colin, it had to mean something.

There was only one reason the map was so important to Uncle Colin that he would keep it in his pocket forever.

"If we're going to find this treasure—"

Pierce motioned for Youssef to keep his voice low. "We need to figure out what this is a map of," Pierce finished for him.

A beer finally appeared in front of Youssef who gave a clap of his hands and grinned. "Finally!"

The liquid in the tankard sloshed over onto the table as the boy placed it down, causing him to jerk his hand and send droplets of ale flying. Pierce quickly grabbed the map and glared at the youth.

"Looks more like a hill fort to me," said the boy. "Perhaps the one at Crosland."

Pierce looked from the boy to the map and then back at him. His eyes opened wider, with the pink splotches on his cheeks reappearing. He quickly ran away, disappearing among the patrons.

Pierce shoved back his chair, the legs squeaking across the

floorboards.

"Where are you going?" Youssef asked, his gaze fixed upon the ale as he brought it to his lips.

"That boy knows something, and I'm going to find out what."

Chapter Two

Why oh why did she have to say anything?

Ginny darted away from the man, skirting around the tables, and twisting her body to dodge a customer who was flailing his arm in excitement as he talked to his companion. What part of remaining hidden had she forgotten?

She glanced over her shoulder to spot the man in pursuit. Blast.

"Wait a moment," he called.

She ignored him, slipped into the dining room and dashed past a long table of boisterous patrons, too engrossed in their meals and potentially deep in their cups to notice her panic.

Her throat dried as she scanned the room. She swore she felt the tall man bearing down upon her, but she didn't dare pause to look back again. Whatever he wanted with her, she didn't want to know. The plan was to remain hidden as long as possible and getting involved with a man who had danger written all over him was not a sensible idea.

Gaze settling on the small alcove near the door, just big enough to fit her slender frame, Ginny ducked into the shadows and pressed her back against the wall. The cool surface pressed against her spine, and she held her breath.

Seconds later, he appeared in the doorway, scanning the room with sharp eyes. Ginny's pulse quickened as he stepped closer, his gaze sweeping over the alcove.

She closed her eyes, praying he wouldn't see her. Several

heartbeats passed.

Unable to resist peeling open one eye, then the other, she saw the wolfish grin cross his lips.

Her heart leapt into her throat. Before he could cut his way across the room, she shot from her hiding spot and headed for the rear door toward the courtyard.

Bright sunlight temporarily blinded her as she flung open the door, she put a hand to her cap and headed for the stables.

"Hey, wait!"

By God, the man was persistent. She should have ignored the intriguing drawing he possessed, should have kept her opinions to herself like Mother always wanted. There was nothing worse than a woman expressing an opinion, according to Mama. Even when the opinion was fact, apparently. And Ginny had been fairly certain what she had seen was the stone circle. After all, she'd spent enough time there as a child to recognize the shape of it.

Not that any of that mattered.

Ginny pushed herself forward, aware strands of hair slipped out of her disguise as she raced across the cobbles. She heard the man's footsteps pounding against the stone as he chased after her.

Her breaths came in short gasps, misting in the cool winter air, as she reached the stable doors, wrenching them open and diving inside. The smell of hay and manure filled her nostrils as she tried to catch her breath.

A hand curled around her arm, hauling her to a halt.

She looked at the barn, where the horses were silhouetted against the shadows inside. She quickly returned her gaze to the man, his features barely visible due to the strong sunlight that haloed him.

"Let me be," she protested and tugged against his hold.

He resisted her tug with a strong grip. I only want to ask—"

The cap slipped from her head as she pulled again. Hair spilled over her shoulders and his hold on her loosened.

"What the—"

She didn't let him utter anything else and used his surprise to free herself and shove past him. This was a disaster. She'd been here mere days and she'd already ruined her disguise. She came to a stop by the rear door to the kitchen, only to find it locked. She slammed a hand against the wood and turned with a sigh, resigned to her fate.

The man approached as though walking up to a skittish mare, hands raised in surrender.

"You're a girl."

"Obviously."

He smirked. "Hardly obvious."

She supposed he referred to her lack of curves and plain features. A man like him probably rarely bothered to even look at a woman like her, let alone speak to them. Stubble grazed a jaw that one would say was cut perfectly were it not for the tiny pale scar upon his chin. Another scar added intrigue just above a brow and she counted one more red mark upon his upper cheek —a fairly recent graze, she imagined.

When she added the scars to the broad shoulders, the inked mark she spied peeking out from his jacket sleeve, and the dark golden hair that needed a cut, she could only come to one conclusion.

This man was trouble.

And trouble had found out the truth about her.

Ginny's mind raced for a solution as the man stepped closer, studying her with a mix of curiosity and amusement. She drew herself up to her full height and tried to look imposing, but the effect was lost as her hair fell in her face.

"What do you want?" she demanded.

He raised an eyebrow. "I was about to ask you the same thing. What's a girl doing dressed like a boy and sneaking around like a spy?"

"I—" she hesitated, unsure of how much to reveal. "I have my reasons."

"Care to share them?"

"No."

He took another step forward and Ginny instinctively backed away, bumping into the inn wall. Something in his eyes made her heart race even faster.

"The map" —He waved the piece of paper she'd spotted on the table in front of her— "what do you know of it?"

"I told you, it's the stone circle at Crosland. Now if you'll excuse me..." She inched sideways along the wall, but he stalked her movements.

"How could you know that?"

She rolled her eyes. Of course he didn't trust her at her word. No man ever had. How could she possibly know more than them when she had never studied history at university or tutored under a renowned expert?

"It's rather obvious, and I do not think that's a map."

He lifted the paper,

"What makes you say that?"

"The lack of any identifiable landmarks for one. It's just a sketch of a pattern, and that pattern matches the shape of the stone circle. I've seen similar drawings of it before."

He studied her for a moment longer, his blue gaze sharp and delving before he stuffed the sketch into his jacket pocket. "How do you know so much about the circle?"

"I grew up here." Ginny peered behind him at her hat sitting forlornly on the cobbles.

"That doesn't explain the disguise."

She met his gaze and straightened her shoulders. "I needed to remain hidden. It's none of your concern."

He leaned in, invading her personal space. "It is my concern if you're somehow involved in whatever that map leads to."

"And why would you care? What's in it for you?"

He straightened, a devilish grin crossing his lips. "That's for me to know and for you to find out."

Ginny felt a thrill run through her at the challenge in his words. She had always been a curious creature, and the mystery of this man and the map was almost too enticing to ignore.

"I really must—" She stepped sideways, and he moved in

front of her. She went the other way, but he blocked her path again.

"I want your help."

She blinked at him a few times. "My help?"

"You clearly have knowledge of the area and I need a guide."

"I have a job."

"As a kitchen boy." His eyes crinkled. "I could pay you well and you wouldn't have to be running around in trousers."

"I don't need money and the trousers are fine," she lied.

"What do you need?" He stepped close, making her aware of their height difference, stifling the air in her lungs.

"To get my hat," she muttered, "now if you'll excuse me—"

He moved so close she could do nothing but step back against the wall. "Please," she said, the word so fragile she hated herself for the weakness behind it.

"I'll make you a deal."

"I don't—"

"I won't reveal your identity if you come and work for me."

Ginny searched his gaze. She didn't know this man or his intentions behind being here. Everything about him set her body on alert. She'd be a fool to agree.

She sucked in a breath, lips parted as she eyed this stranger who had the audacity to order her about. "You cannot blackmail me into helping you."

The responding smirk told her otherwise.

∞∞∞

The lift of her chin made his lips quirk. Pierce seldom met such courage in such a short package.

"I am not blackmailing you," Pierce said, his voice low and smooth. "I am simply offering you a choice. Help me and I'll keep your secret. Refuse and I can't guarantee your anonymity."

He framed her with both of his arms, his body so close he felt the warmth of her competing against the cold air. It was easy to see how she had got away with her disguise. Fair lashes and softly curving cheeks meant she looked more like a boy than a grown woman. Were it not for the extremely long lengths of pale hair, he might never have known she was a woman.

"I can quite easily throw you over my shoulder, take you into the inn, and reveal who you are."

Her cheeks paled and he almost regretted the threat until her chin jutted out and she stared up at him.

"You wouldn't dare."

"Try me." He kept her pinned.

Threatening women was not exactly a habit of Pierce's, but he'd been through plenty of negotiations that had turned violent in his travels. Treasure hunting was not exactly the most peaceful of occupations after all.

He doubted this woman would swing at him or test his resolve, though. For whatever reason, she wanted to remain in hiding and he didn't much care why. All he knew was that she had figured out what the map—or sketch—was in mere seconds. He and Youssef would have been studying it for days without her.

For several moments, her chin remained in position, her pale green eyes filled with anger. He held her gaze and kept his posture firm.

Finally, she let out a defeated sigh and looked away. "Fine," she muttered. "What do you need me to do?"

Pierce released her and stepped back, feeling the slight loss of warmth from her absence.

"I need a guide," he said. "Someone who knows the area and can lead me to the stone circle."

"That's all?"

"I'm not a monster," he said, easing back from the wall. "I just need a guide. And I promise, once we've found what we're looking for, I'll leave you alone."

Her brow puckered. "Why should I believe you?"

"You don't have to. But I have a feeling you're curious enough to want to find out what this map leads to."

"It's a sketch," she said bluntly.

"Maybe, maybe not."

"You cannot tell anyone who I am."

He shrugged. "I don't know who you are."

"But of course."

"But of course? Am I meant to know the name of every person in disguise I meet?"

She put her hands to his chest and shoved past him to retrieve the floppy cap waiting on the cobbles. As she stuffed her reams of hair into the hat, Pierce found himself missing the way the long silky lengths framed her soft cheeks.

"I only meant a man like you would have no curiosity as to why I might be dressed as a boy." She straightened her shirtsleeves.

"A man like me?" He stalked her footsteps as she made her way back to the inn.

She paused at the closed door and turned to look at him. "A man like you," she confirmed. "Handsome, confident, completely assured of his place in the world."

Pierce knew what he looked like, knew the few scars and the rugged appearance never hurt his chances when it came to women, though he'd never been that interested in putting the affect to full use. He'd been too busy seeking out adventure and digging in the dirt to worry about whether he might be able to find himself a wife.

A pang jarred through his chest.

He'd also been too busy to take care of his family.

"I'm not a complete ignoramus," he countered, though he wasn't certain that was true. Since he was a boy, once he set his mind to something, he sort of forgot everything else.

She snorted and the sound only made him more annoyed, even if it should have amused him coming from this boyish woman.

"What's your name then?"

She flicked her gaze up and down him, her lips curving. "Do you really think I'm going to tell you?"

"I can hardly call you 'boy' now can I?"

Her lips pursed. "What's your name?"

There was no reason for him to lie. After all, he wasn't the one in hiding. Yet he wasn't sure he wanted to tell her his name. She might not recognize him, but he was the subject of many a news article about his adventures with the occasional mention in the scandal sheets. None of it was unflattering as such and he imagined it would only seal the impression she had of him.

Why he cared, he did not know, but he offered a hand and said, "Pierce."

She repeated his name, glancing at his extended hand before placing her own in it. Despite the cold weather and her work at the inn, her hand was still soft and warm to the touch. This wasn't the hand of someone who worked for a living. He stared at her with curiosity. What the devil could have happened to her to make her come all the way out to the middle of the countryside and disguise herself as a boy?

He shoved aside the thoughts as she shook his hand vigorously and with surprising strength. He wanted to keep his secrets and she wanted to keep hers. It was better that way.

"Ginny," she said.

"Just Ginny?"

"Just Ginny," she confirmed.

"Well, Just Ginny. I want you to take me to the stone circle tomorrow. Think you can take some time off?"

Ginny released a long, audible breath and nodded. "I can manage that."

"Perfect." He flashed a grin. "I'll see you here tomorrow."

Her eyes flashed briefly, her cheeks turning a mottled pink shade that Pierce couldn't deny he enjoyed. If she was going to make judgements about him from a mere first impression, he didn't mind riling her one bit—so long as she did what he asked and helped her find the treasure that could secure his family's future once and for all.

Chapter Three

Perhaps he wasn't coming. Ginny pressed the door open enough so she could just peer through the gap at the increasingly busy taproom of the inn. It was nearly lunchtime and there was no sign of this adventuring duke-to-be. Maybe he was lounging about at his family's luxurious estate, bathing in adoration from visiting ladies—an estate which apparently housed many treasures and boasted acres and acres of land. She'd never visited the Marbury Estate as it was a little too far from Oakfield for a young girl to travel but she could easily picture him enjoying all the trappings of inherited wealth.

She eased out a slightly shaky breath. If he didn't turn up within the next hour, she would conclude he had changed his mind about wanting her help.

Which was a good thing.

Was it not?

She scowled at herself. Of course it was a good thing. She didn't want to help such an arrogant, demanding man. He wanted to blackmail her into helping for goodness' sakes!

"Of course such a man would go immediately to blackmail," she muttered to herself. Since their meeting yesterday—if one could call him chasing after her and essentially threatening her as meeting—she had discovered he wasn't just any man running around with a sketch of the stone circle.

He was the son of a duke.

And not just any son of a duke, but an infamous one. Most sons of dukes had their fair share of news written about them but according to several of the patrons she'd spoken to yesterday, Pierce was known for seeking out treasures in the far flung reaches of the world.

She should have known. Everything from the way he carried himself to the way he tossed about demands had indicated him being a man who was used to getting what he wished but the slightly scruffy appearance and the scars had confused her.

Ginny pressed her nose back to the gap in the door as more customers entered the room. "And what man *doesn't* think he can get whatever they wish?" she whispered.

After her encounter with her fiancé and some of the demanding customers at the inn, she was beginning to conclude all men wandered around expecting to get exactly what they wanted at all times.

"You cannot hide here all day, you know."

Ginny whirled, a hand to her chest as her sister entered the kitchen from the rear door. She wore a beautifully cut pelisse lined with pink stitching that flattered her copper hair. Few people who looked at her would think Maisie capable of running a successful inn. Right now, she looked very much like the wife of a viscountess.

"I won't," Ginny promised. "I know you're busy with Apollo and you need—"

Maisie raised a hand. "I don't need you to do anything, Ginny. We're quite well staffed at this point."

Ginny held back a sarcastic retort about being glad she was useful. Her sister had done her a great favor letting her remain here in hiding.

"You know," her sister said, "I can get Apollo to throw a few threats around. Scare this man off."

Ginny imagined Maisie's huge fiancé squaring up to Pierce easily enough, but she shook her head. Apollo had suffered a reputation that was entirely unfair in his youth and the last thing she wanted was for him to dent the progress he'd made in proving himself to be quite the philanthropist.

"You've done enough."

Maisie paused halfway through doing up the buttons of her gloves. "Are you certain you do not wish to go with the man, Ginny? I know what you're like."

"I might have a passion for the past but that does not mean I am inclined to give my aid to such a man. Mrs. Weaver showed me the scandal sheets from last summer. He's only in it for the fame and fortune and I will not let him use Oakfield like that."

"Just be careful please." Her sister's mouth thinned. "I hate the thought of you running around the countryside with a man like that."

"If he even arrives, I shall tell him in no uncertain terms that I shall not be aiding him. I doubt he'll really follow through with his threats anyway."

Maisie gave her a troubled look then nodded. "If you're certain."

"Go." Ginny turned from the door and made a shooing motion to her sister. "I can manage a scoundrel like him."

After all, she'd slapped her fiancé, stolen his carriage, lied to her family and disguised herself as a boy. Refusing to aid an arrogant, powerful man would be a doddle.

She waved her sister off out of the rear door and turned around.

She screamed.

Pierce stood in the kitchen, arms folded, no more refined looking than yesterday with no cravat and a greatcoat open to reveal a thick jacket hanging over a loose shirt underneath and no waistcoat.

He grinned broadly. "I prefer to be called a rogue."

"I know full well what you are." She kept the kitchen table between them, aware of the tremor in her voice. "And *who* you are."

"Someone has been doing their research I see?" Pierce smirked. "You do know not everything you read is true."

"Oh so you do not seek out treasures and sell them on for great profit?"

He lifted a shoulder.

"And you certainly haven't gained fame through such pursuits to the point you are known as the Daredevil Duke?"

"I always rather liked that name, though I think it paints me in a slightly more reckless light than necessary and I'm not actually a duke."

"What would you prefer?" She inched around the table when he began to move forward, keeping the distance between them. "Mercenary perhaps? Or charlatan?"

"There's nothing wrong with discovering the mysteries of the world."

Ginny folded her arms as though it could provide her with a shield against this man when a table clearly wasn't enough. The sun shone brightly in through the windows, bathing the man in its warm light. His golden hair gleamed, and it brought out the burnished quality of his skin.

"So you know all about me," he murmured, a wicked glint in his eyes. "Well…" He paused, meeting her gaze head on. "I know all about you too, Genevieve Beaufort."

∞∞∞

The way her eyes widened made Pierce's triumphant grin widen. It hadn't taken many questions about a Ginny from Oakfield for him to discover who she was. No one had connected the innkeeper's sister to the boy working at the inn yet, though.

What he still didn't quite know was why she was in hiding. Frankly, it didn't really matter. All he knew was he wanted her help. Youssef didn't understand his obsession with having the woman aid him, but Youssef didn't understand a lot of things Pierce did.

Actually, neither did he. All he knew was there was more to this woman than a disguise and ridiculously long hair, and his gut told him she would be extremely useful to them.

Pierce never, ever ignored his gut.

Ginny moved around the table. "So you know my name?

What does that matter?"

"It doesn't. That's if you're still intending to help me." He paused when he spotted a flash of ginger fur in the corner of the room. "Is that cat eating cheese?"

"She likes cheese."

Shaking his head, he returned his attention to Ginny. "Are you going to help me or not?"

"I'm assuming you're after some sort of treasure."

"Assume all you wish."

"I do not agree with treasure hunting. Historical artifacts should be preserved for all to see."

Pierce snorted. "You sound like a museum curator, not someone who's passionate about the past."

"I am passionate about the past," Ginny retorted. "But that doesn't mean I condone looting and pillaging historical sites!"

"I don't pillage," Pierce replied. "I discover. And if that discovery happens to come with a reward, then so be it."

"You're nothing more than a thief," Ginny said, her eyes flashing. "You have no respect for the people who came before us, for the lives they lived, the stories they told. All you care about is your own fame and fortune."

"That's not true," Pierce said, taking a step closer to her. "I care about the past just as much as you do. But I don't see the harm in profiting from my discoveries."

"You're still taking something that doesn't belong to you," she shot back.

"You cannot tell me your curiosity isn't piqued." He took a few more steps around the table toward her. "You want to help me, Ginny."

She folded her arms. "No, I do not, and you cannot make me. No one will believe you when you tell them there's a woman disguised as a boy in some village no one cares about."

"No, but they'll believe me when I show them."

He glanced her over, unable to picture what she would look like out of the trousers and shirt and in some sort of frothy gown.

He did, however, have the briefest flash of an image of naked skin and long pale hair.

"What do you—"

With two swift strides, he closed the gap between them, scooped her up with ease and tossed her over his shoulder. She squealed.

Hoping the bustle from the taproom covered the sound, he kept his grip firm on the wriggling woman and shoved open the rear door of the kitchen with a boot.

"Put me down," she cried, fists pounding upon his back. "Help!"

Pierce winced. She wasn't the strongest of women, but he'd have a few bruises tomorrow he'd wager. Still, it would be worth it.

He paused in front of the horses and ignored Youssef's surprised expression as he set Ginny down on the ground. Her attempts at wriggling from his hold swiftly weakened and she glared at him.

"You cannot just cart me about like some sack of grain!"

The fury staining her cheeks was quite something. He should have known a woman willing to disguise herself as a boy would have quite the fight in her.

"*I* can do what I wish," he said, keeping her arms pinned at her side as she squirmed again. "I'm not the one in hiding."

"Help!" she screamed once more. "This bastard is kidnapping me!"

Pierce twisted her and clamped a hand over her mouth, pinning her firmly against his body with his free arm. Her breaths were hot and furious against his palm.

"Mmppph!"

"You have two choices, Genevieve Beaufort. Help me or be carted into that inn and have your true identity revealed to everyone."

She sagged in his hold, and he tried to ignore how soft she was against him for someone so unshapely.

"Once I've shown everyone in there you're a woman, I'll be

certain to write a few letters to a few newspapers and see quite what or who you are hiding from."

"Mmmphh."

"Will you help me then?"

"Mmmphh."

Slowly he peeled his hand away from her mouth. "Well, then?"

"You're a bastard."

"Is that a yes?"

Ginny's shoulders dropped. "Yes."

"Excellent." He released her carefully, preparing himself for a slap across the face or perhaps a kick to the shins from this furious bundle of a woman.

She whirled around to face him, her gaze ablaze. "I despise you."

Pierce chuckled. "Sweeting, you can hate me all you want. There's plenty of people who feel exactly the same." He motioned to the horse and his friend who just shook his head in dismay. "Can you show us the way to the stone circle?"

"Fine," she muttered. "Let's go before the weather breaks."

Youssef swung his gaze between Pierce and Ginny then nudged Pierce with an elbow. "Kidnapping people, Pierce? That's a new low for you."

"It's not kidnap."

"It's not," Ginny agreed, and Youssef's brows lifted. "It's blackmail."

"Oh good," Youssef said dryly. "We can add blackmail to our list of misdeeds."

Pierce shrugged. "Just another day in the life of a treasure hunter."

"Mercenary," Ginny corrected as she climbed up onto the horse and swung her leg over like she had been riding astride her entire life.

Youssef gave Pierce a look that told him his friend didn't think having Ginny with them was going to be worth the effort. They needed her, though. He just knew that somehow Ginny would be the key to them succeeding where his uncle had failed.

Chapter Four

Ginny gripped the saddle as the horse's hooves pounded a steady rhythm beneath her. Acutely aware of Pierce's muscular arms caging her in, his broad chest pressed against her back, she forced herself to focus on the gentle rise of the grassy slope leading to the stone circle.

To her left, Pierce's friend Youssef rode alongside on a bay mare and when she glanced at him he flashed a slightly apologetic smile. At least *he* was on her side. Perhaps this man, with kindly looking eyes and a white-flecked beard would persuade his friend to leave Ginny be.

Or perhaps Pierce would give up on her once she showed him the stone circle. She'd spent many a day there during her childhood, weaving between the rocks and twirling her skirts while she pretended to be from some ancient civilization. Her father always said she had a curious imagination and he'd often taken time away from running the inn to indulge her curiosity with visits to old castles and other historical sites.

A deep sigh escaped her lips. She missed the companionship of someone who shared her same passion for exploring the secrets hidden in historical artifacts.

Sadly, no one else in her family seemed to appreciate her curiosity about the past. Her mother and sisters were intent on making their mark on society and her brother was too wrapped up in his own affairs. She'd thought her fiancé would be the answer to it all. He was the key to her fulfilling her dreams of at the very least aiding in the understanding of history.

But it wasn't to be.

So here she was, sitting here like a good little girl in front of this man who kidnapped her, this man who didn't care a fig about the past, this man who thought of her as little more than a trinket he could cart about.

She bit her lip. She should have fought harder, but he'd made it clear he would let everyone know who she was. The last thing she needed was her horrible fiancé tracking her down.

Ginny straightened to ease the ache in her lower back. Trying to keep a sliver of distance between her and Pierce made every muscle in her body hurt as she swayed in the saddle.

A stilted cough from behind her drew her attention back to the man she was unfortunately stuck with.

"I will do whatever I can to aid you in finding whatever it is you're looking for," she muttered. "Just don't expect me to do any digging."

"Treasure hunting is so rarely anything to do with digging," he said, chuckling. "Isn't that right, Youssef?"

"Oh yes." His friend nodded. "More often than not, we find ourselves in dank, dark caves or tunnels full of spiderwebs."

Ginny scowled. "And you enjoy doing this?"

Youssef shrugged, his lips curving. "Better than what I used to be doing before I met Pierce."

"What was that?"

"You do not want to know," Pierce said, his voice low.

"But what—"

"You do *not* want to know," he repeated.

Youssef's grin widened when she looked at him. She shook her head. Quite how she had found herself in this situation, she did not know, but she could safely conclude running away without a moment's thought had been the start of it all. What other options she had, though, she had yet to figure out.

Soon the ancient stone circle came into view, high atop a mound, just a ring of grassy mounds with weathered rocks peeking out. A heavy silence hung in the air.

"Remarkable," breathed Youssef. "I never would have

recognized this place as the circle depicted on the map." He looked at Ginny. "You've got quite the eye, Miss Beaufort."

Ginny's cheeks warmed. Pierce grunted behind her, but she wasn't certain why. She dismounted before Pierce could aid her down. She climbed up the slope and reverently approached the nearest mound. Fingers trailing over the moss-eaten rock, she imagined the hands that had placed it there thousands of years ago. This hallowed place deserved preservation, not the careless plundering Pierce intended.

"It doesn't look like the map to me," Pierce said, hands on hips as he surveyed the area.

"It's a sketch." Ginny pressed her lips together and gestured to the stones. "But by all means, let your ignorance guide us."

Pierce raised an eyebrow. "And how many ancient treasures have you discovered, sweeting?"

"This site is about more than treasure," she said tightly. "This place could reveal so much about the ancient people who lived here. We owe it to the future to preserve their legacy."

She gestured to the weathered stones. "Can't you imagine standing here thousands of years ago, watching people gathering for rituals, hearing chants echoing across the hills?" Her voice grew soft with wonder. "It's a portal to another world, forgotten by time. We walk in the footsteps of our ancestors."

"Very poetic." Pierce rolled his eyes.

Youssef came to Ginny's side after hitching the horses to a nearby tree. "I understand what you mean, Miss Beaufort. I come from Egypt where we have towering pyramids and ancient tombs. It's humbling to walk amongst them."

"I imagine you do not appreciate men digging through those tombs and stealing its treasures much, either," she said, her gaze fixed on Pierce who looked more amused than insulted at her jab.

"This is hardly a great pyramid," Pierce said, moving close.

"But it is just as important," she shot back and took a step forward.

Youssef moved in between them. "You are right, Miss Beaufort. I do not enjoy seeing my ancestors' history taken from where it belongs, but Pierce has no intention of doing any damage."

"He'll still be taking something that does not belong to him." She set her hands to her hips. "If, that is, you even know what it is you're looking for. Is that sketch your only clue?"

"It's a map," Pierce said firmly, "and I'll know what I'm hunting for when I find it."

Youssef leaned in. "His uncle brought him up on tales of a huge treasure hoard in this very county but whether it was a..." he frowned "...flight of fancy, who can say? All we know is that the map Pierce holds was with his uncle until the last moment so it must be important."

"So I've been kidnapped because of tall tales?"

"Come now, Miss Beaufort," Pierce said with a grin. "You cannot tell me you are not at least curious."

Ginny issued a long breath. She loathed that he could read her so clearly already. It would not make keeping her secrets from him any easier.

∞ ∞ ∞

Pierce watched Ginny move carefully among the weathered pillars, brow furrowed as she compared the positioning of them to the map. He'd begun to think bringing the irritating woman with them was a mistake, especially since Youssef kept wasting his time with trying to be all pleasant to her. As near as he could tell, pleasantries were most certainly wasted on her.

What Ginny wanted, he did not know, and that was frustrating in itself. Usually woman rather flung themselves at him. Once they heard all about his adventures, he found himself drowning in their attentions. But not Ginny. No, she was different. She was stubborn, opinionated, and entirely unwilling to give in to his charm.

A while later, Pierce sat on the ground, back against one of the stout stones and studied the weary look on Ginny's face.

She rubbed the back of her neck with a hand and rolled her neck. "We could be at this for days."

Pierce ignored the strange desire to stand and ease away the aches in her muscles with his own hands.

"We'll head back in time for supper." He reached for his canteen and took a long pull of water then stood and walked over to offer her a drink.

She took it cautiously and put it to her mouth. He blinked at the sight of soft lips curving around it and the way her throat moved when she swallowed. Pretending to be a boy was the perfect disguise for this plain woman, but he had to admit, there wasn't much masculinity in those lips.

She caught his gaze, a crease forming between her brows, and he looked away swiftly.

Handing back the water, she took a step toward the nearest stone. "Perhaps if we—" Her foot dislodged a stone and she stumbled.

Pierce jumped forward and grabbed her arm to steady her.

"Careful," he murmured.

Their faces were suddenly close, the scent of soap lingering in the air about her. Acute awareness of the warmth of her sizzled through him. Pierce froze, able to feel the racing of her pulse under his fingers. Her gaze met his, wide with surprise. For a breathless moment the world narrowed down to just the two of them.

Then Ginny pulled back abruptly, a faint blush on her cheeks. "I can manage on my own, thank you," she said crisply, though her voice was unsteady.

Pierce nodded and cleared his throat, trying to ignore the ghost of her touch that lingered. "Of course."

He stepped back, ignoring the look Youssef gave him from his spot on the other side of the mound, and let Ginny take the lead in examining the weathered stones.

"Did your uncle say anything else of this treasure?" She waved the map at him. "This might well be useless."

"It was his most prized possession. He wouldn't have had it

upon him had it not been important."

She gave him a doubtful look. "He would not be the first man to chase a treasure that does not exist."

"It had better exist."

"Oh, more threats. But of course."

He hissed out a breath. "That's not what I meant."

He removed his hat, shoved a hand through his hair, and set it back on his head. She could have no idea what it was like being the heir to a dukedom. Hell, here was a woman content to run from her problems whatever those were. He wasn't able to do the same.

At least not any longer. He'd been away too long, avoided responsibility for too many years. His family was paying the price for that and if he did not find this hoard, he wasn't certain he could save them from his own failings.

"I just want to find this damned treasure," he muttered.

"Well, we need more than this sketch."

"Map."

"Perhaps there's nothing to find," Ginny said. She gestured at the weathered stones. "This place is ancient and maybe if there was something here, it has already been taken."

"It has to be here."

"Unless you are willing to dig through every inch of this mound, I do not see how we can find it." Ginny shook her head and set her hands to her hips. "This is a fool's errand."

"If I have to dig every inch of this place, I will."

Her chin lifted. "I would never let you. This place deserves respect."

"I respect it well enough."

She made a dismissive noise. "I do not think a man like you can ever truly respect history."

"An expert on history *and* men now are we?"

She met his gaze. "I've encountered enough men like you to understand your kind quite well."

He raised an eyebrow. "My kind?"

"Arrogant, entitled, and only interested in what benefits

them."

"I see." Pierce leaned in, close enough that he could see the flecks of green in her brown eyes. "And what kind of men do you prefer, sweeting?"

Ginny's eyes narrowed. "The kind who understand the value of history and respect it enough to leave it be."

"If the mysteries of the past remained buried, how would we know anything of the past?"

"Oh do not pretend this is all for historical research. This is to fill your pocketbook, nothing more."

The sum that a hoard as large as his uncle had talked about would certainly do more than that and he couldn't deny it was the driving force behind his desire to find it.

"I am not here *only* for the wealth."

"No, probably the fame too."

"You know nothing of me."

"I know all about you." She jabbed a finger to his chest. "You come here, with your map that may or may not be accurate, and you expect to find something that has been hidden for centuries. You do not care about the consequences." She jabbed again. "You do not care about the history of this place. You only care about what you can gain from it."

He grabbed her finger before she could take another shot at him and held it firmly. "Let us not start making assumptions about one another or I might be tempted to fulfill some of them."

"If you reveal me, I will have no reason to aid you anymore."

"As far as I can tell, you haven't proven your worth yet anyway." He offered a slanted smile as her chest rose and fell rapidly. "I probably made a mistake bringing you along. Clearly, your knowledge of the place is not what I hoped."

"I spent most of my childhood here," she protested. "And no one has studied the history of Oakfield like I have."

"But of course. It seems I have happened upon an expert historian disguised as a boy. Pray tell, sweeting, where might I read some of your research? Do you have a book published perhaps? Or maybe you will be giving a talk in London soon?"

"Why you—"

Youssef approached. "It's been a long morning. Should we perhaps take a break?" He smiled at Ginny and offered her his arm. "What do you think, Miss Beaufort?"

She glanced at Youssef, then at Pierce, then back to Youssef. "Yes, I think that might a good idea." Ginny took his arm. "But you must call me Ginny."

Pierce tightened his jaw as the pair made their way back down the hill, arm in arm. The woman was maddening. One moment she was spitting fire at him, the next she was leaning close to Youssef and talking sweetly to him as though they were close friends sharing secrets.

He heaved out a frustrated sigh. Letting her rile him was pointless and he shouldn't allow his emotions to get the better of him. He needed to stay focused if he was going to find the hoard and save his family from certain ruin.

Chapter Five

They arrived back at the inn in time for supper as promised. Ginny's stomach grumbled at the scent of warm bread mixed with the slight tang of ale. She craved something stronger than a beer. Whiskey perhaps. Her father had often allowed her a little sip on cold nights, though she wasn't cold right now.

With Pierce's arms still surrounding her and his firm chest against her back, she was actually entirely too warm.

Perhaps strong liquor wouldn't be a good idea. She needed to maintain her guard around this man. Here was a man used to getting whatever he wanted. She wasn't going to allow him to leave a path of destruction in his wake as he searched for this treasure.

Whether he would really reveal her or not, she realized now she had no choice but to aid him, if only to persuade him to do something noble with the treasure.

If it even existed, of course.

She ignored his outstretched hand after he dismounted and swung her leg over the horse quickly. Too quickly. Her other leg caught on the stirrup, and she fell forward, her face almost colliding with the dirt. But strong arms caught her and pulled her back up, her body flush against Pierce's. She could feel his breath on her neck and shuddered.

"Careful there," he said, amusement in his voice.

Ginny pulled away from him and brushed the dirt off her trousers. "I don't need your help," she snapped.

"Given the situation you are in, I'm not certain that's true."

"You know nothing of my situation."

And it would remain that way. The fewer people who knew why she was in hiding the better. With any luck, Horace would be heading back to Scotland and as soon as she knew he was gone, she could return to her old life.

Her old, *boring* life.

Marrying Horace was meant to open doors that remained firmly shut to women. He'd made it clear those doors were not only going to be closed but firmly bolted too. Being his wife would be even more restricting than her current life.

"I might be able to help, you know," Pierce said as he led the horse into the stables and handed it over to the stable boy. "I am something of an important person, if you recall."

"Really?" she said dryly. "I had no idea."

Though, truth be told, despite his arrogance, if she had not been told he was the heir to a dukedom, she'd never have known. He didn't dress like a duke, and he certainly didn't behave like one. She'd only ever glanced at one in her entire life, but the man had been primped and polished and held court as though he were the Prince Regent himself. She had no reason to think other dukes were any different.

Ginny looked at Pierce. Perhaps she wasn't the only one in disguise. She had an inkling there was something more to this man than his brash arrogance—something she didn't want to think too much about. She should conserve her brain power for far more interesting things like finding this treasure.

As they made their way through the inn to a table, Ginny couldn't help but notice the way men and women alike turned to stare at Pierce. He commanded attention without even trying.

She rolled her eyes when he grinned at the women who batted their eyelashes at him and nodded in acknowledgement to the men who tipped their hats in his direction. Ginny tried her best to ignore it all, but it wasn't easy. She was used to blending in, not standing out.

Youssef either didn't notice or didn't care about the looks

they received. She imagined his friend was used to such a reaction. She glanced his way and Youssef just shrugged and smiled.

"Is it always like this?" she asked, leaning in.

"Oh sometimes it's worse, especially if we're in London."

"I do not know how you tolerate it," she muttered.

In fact, she didn't know how the affable man tolerated Pierce at all. She'd known him a day and wanted to strangle him at least a dozen times already.

"English folks seem to derive pleasure for idolizing people." He chuckled as Pierce fended off the attentions of a young, giggling lady. "I never understood it much, but I reckon the grim weather does something to your brains. Not enough sunshine."

"I wonder how it is you cope with being in such a rainy country. Do you not miss home?"

"Well, if I miss it, all I need to do is visit London. One fellow even has a pyramid as his tomb."

Ginny laughed. "We do have a tendency for mimicry here. I imagine we can blame the weather for that too."

They finally worked their way past the admirers and Ginny led them into the private dining room. Pierce waited for her to sit, and she motioned furiously for him to sit first.

"I'm a boy remember and most certainly not an important one," she hissed.

He blinked a few times then nodded. "How could I forget?"

She very much doubted he really saw her as a woman. In some ways, she made a better boy. Her features seemed more suited to the simple aesthetics expected of men, though if she studied Pierce, she struggled to see anything simple in his features. The lamplight illuminated his sharp bone structure, revealing the tiny flashes of pale scars, and the stubble on his jaw had grown thicker. This man was *nothing* like the duke she'd spied at a ball once.

"Is there something on my face?" he asked, brushing his hand across his jaw.

"No. Nothing," she quickly replied, shaking her head. "I was just, uh, wondering when you were going to tell me more about this treasure or are you worried I might try to find it myself?"

Pierce leaned back in his chair, regarding her with tilted lips. "I think you would have a hard time finding it without me," he said, his tone teasing. "But I suppose I can share some details with you."

"Considering you have blackmailed me into helping you, I think it's only fair."

"Well—"

Ginny didn't notice her sister approach, until she came to stand in front of the table. Her fiancé Apollo lingered in the doorway, his arms folded and surrounded by the perfect air of menace. Ginny almost laughed.

"So this is the man who has been threatening you, Ginny?" Maisie asked, propping her hands on her hips. "Shall I toss him out now or after he has issued a groveling apology?"

∞∞∞

The redheaded woman eyed him and were it not for the flash of fury in her eyes, Pierce wouldn't have figured out the connection between her and Ginny.

"You're her sister," Pierce stated.

"Yes, and I will not allow you to use her in any such manner."

He looked toward the man lingering in the doorway, his jaw set firm, even as he showed no sign of joining the fray. Whoever he was had probably concluded Ginny's sister could manage the situation herself.

Ginny lifted a hand. "Maisie, I told you I could handle this."

"You've been gone all day, you're covered in dirt, and you've been in the company of this...this..."

"Rogue," Pierce finished for her.

"Blaggard," Youssef offered.

Pierce glared at his friend. "Thank you, Youssef."

He grinned. "You're welcome."

Ginny rose from her chair and took her sister to one side. He didn't catch their whispered conversation, but the occasional insult reached his ears.

"One day, Pierce," Youssef said, "we shall go somewhere where you don't have women fighting over you."

"Never."

He looked toward the women, watching as Ginny's sister marched out of the room. Ginny sighed and came back to join them at the table.

"Is everything well?" he asked.

"Maisie means well, but I'm her younger sister and she's worried for me. She thinks I'm a delicate flower or something."

"Delicate flower?" Pierce repeated. "You don't strike me as a delicate flower."

"Why thank you," she said.

"More of like a thistle perhaps?" He paused. "Because you're prickly."

She gave him an icy stare. "If you're going to insult me, perhaps call me a weed, because I'm able to survive the worst."

"And is the worst happening currently?" Pierce leaned in. "Is that why you are hiding out with your sister disguised as a boy?"

"This is her inn. She runs it with her fiancé."

"The menacing looking chap?"

"He's not as tough as he looks." Ginny hesitated. "I probably shouldn't be telling you that."

"I have no intention of starting any fights," Pierce said and thrust a thumb at Youssef. "That's what he's for."

"I thought I was here for my personality and dazzling looks," Youssef protested.

Ginny swung her gaze between them and smiled slightly. Pierce had to admit, he rather liked seeing her smile.

"You still haven't explained why you are here in disguise," he pressed.

She shook her head. "It's a dull story and it doesn't really matter." She jabbed the table with a finger. "What matters is that we eat, and you tell me what else you know of the treasure."

Pierce couldn't prevent a grin slipping across his lips when he recalled all the tales his uncle had furnished him with as a boy—some real and some most certainly false or at the very least exaggerated. The story of the treasure in Oakfield was no lie, though. His uncle had hunted for it until the end of his days and finding it would not only mean saving his family from financial ruin but fulfilling the dream of a man who had taught Pierce there was more to life than stuffy ballrooms and sitting around in gentleman's clubs.

"During the civil war, many castles were sacked and ruined," Pierce began.

"Like Heversham Castle?" Ginny asked.

Of course the woman knew of it. He had to wonder if there was anything of the local history she didn't know and quite why a young woman had such an interest in it. It was hardly a hobby encouraged in young ladies and as near as he could tell, Ginny Beaufort was not as humble as her disguise suggested. Her eloquent speech and excellent knowledge hinted at least a decent education.

He had more important mysteries to solve than why she should wind up dressed as boy and bringing beer to impatient customers, though.

Pierce nodded. "Exactly like Heversham Castle, actually."

"What does that have to do with any treasure?"

"Well, the Royalists knew things were looking dire, and many wealthy nobles began to hide their wealth in case things soured further."

Ginny propped her elbows on the table and rested her chin on her hands. "So this treasure belongs to a Royalist?"

He almost laughed when she shifted forward in her seat like a child waiting to hear their favorite tale.

"Heversham Castle belonged to Lord Robert York, a man of huge wealth."

"And he hid his treasure?" Her brow crinkled. "But why are we not searching the castle?"

"My uncle searched high and low throughout his life, and

you can believe me when I say he would have searched every inch of those ruins," Pierce explained. "But Lord Robert would not have wanted his wealth hidden in the castle in case Cromwell did attack and pull down the walls."

"Which he did." She shook her head. "Blasted man."

"Agreed." Pierce leaned back in his chair as a serving girl brought over ales and he took a sip of his drink. "But Lord Robert was no fool. The story is that he had his wealth moved to safety and hid it where no one would think to look."

Ginny sat forward, eyes shining with an excitement that should have made Pierce uneasy. He only wanted her as a guide, nothing more.

"And where is that?"

"That," Pierce said, "is what we have to find out. The fact is, my uncle believed the treasure never reached its destination."

"How could your uncle even know this?"

He glanced at Youssef who shrugged. "Tell her, Pierce."

"Uncle Colin enjoyed a good drink."

Ginny rolled her eyes. "Wonderful."

"He was drinking with a man one night with the surname of York. The man told him the story of the treasure and how it was thought the men transporting the wealth were either preyed upon or they were greedy and took the treasure for themselves. All that was known was the men vanished and Robert York died in battle not long after."

"If these men took it, they might have spent it all," she pointed out.

"Well, that's what I used to tell Uncle Colin, however, he came to me a few years ago and told me he'd discovered the whereabouts of one of the men entrusted with the wealth and he had been buried in a pauper's grave."

"Hardly a burial worthy of a man with great wealth," she murmured. "But are you really trusting in the tale of a drunkard?"

"No, but I'm trusting my uncle, and I'm trusting this map."

"Sketch," she countered. "Which doesn't mean anything."

"Colin had this upon his person when he died, and Oakfield is on one of the oldest roads in England—a road that leads directly from Heversham Castle."

Her lips pursed. "You're making assumptions."

Pierce tugged the map out of his pocket and laid it out on the table. "He even annotated it." He jabbed it with his finger. "Look,"

Ginny leaned forward. "Oakfield Hoard."

"That's what my uncle called this treasure." He folded the map carefully and eased it back into the inner pocket of his jacket. "This map means something, and we need to figure out what."

A pale brow lifted. "We?"

"Oh, you're accompanying me until we find this treasure, sweeting. Now you know all about it, I'm not letting you out of my sight."

"You're assuming I can take time away from the inn," she pointed out.

"You're the sister—"

She fixed him with a glare and glanced around.

"Very well, the brother of the innkeeper. Of course you can be spared."

Youssef rubbed his hands together as the serving girl returned with three plates, balanced carefully on both arms. "Enough damned treasure talk," he said. "I'm famished.

"Youssef's right." Ginny smiled so sweetly at Youssef that it made Pierce tighten his grip on his ale. He doubted he'd ever be on the receiving end of such a smile. "We cannot think of our next steps on empty stomachs," she said in honeyed tones as though she hadn't been spitting fire at him all day.

He had to wonder if it was all a big mistake bringing her along, but she'd already proven to have great knowledge of the history of the area, and he knew little of Oakfield. He'd travelled enough to know that the knowledge of a local could mean the difference between going home empty-handed or making a discovery that could change everything they know of the world.

And this odd little woman in disguise could well be the key

to ensuring his family's survival.

Chapter Six

"I really do think we should consider taking one of my brother-in-law's horses." Ginny winced, muscles aching, and fingers tired from the grip she had on the pommel in an attempt to avoid touching Pierce at all as she rode with him on his horse.

"This is starting to look silly," she added.

"Says the woman disguised as a boy."

She tensed when he leaned forward, and his baritone whispered in her ear. A shiver tripped down her spine and she blinked a few times in an attempt to keep her attention on the castle. Set high on a hill, it jutted out against the bright blue sky, its ancient stones seeming to glow in the sunlight. A huge expanse of flat land hinted at its past as a moated castle, but the lake had long since been drained, leaving the area about it barren and lifeless.

"Are you ever going to tell me why you are in hiding?"

The fragrance of soap and cologne reached her nostrils. Heat rose in her cheeks, so she forced herself to take deep breaths of cool air. The last thing this arrogant man needed was thinking she was swooning over him.

She'd never swooned over a man, and she didn't plan to start anytime soon. He might be attractive in a devilish, slightly rough way, but there was more to life than one's outward appearance.

There had to be or else her own worth counted for nothing. Being wrapped in plain packaging gave her an opportunity to expand her mind and think of things other than whether she would marry well or attract a handsome husband. She was more than her looks.

But Pierce was not. He relied on them far too much for her liking and she wasn't going to add to the endless admiration he received.

"I have my reasons," she said, keeping her voice steady. "And they are none of your concern."

"Considering you are one of my team now, sweeting, it does concern me a tad."

She glanced back at Youssef. "You count three people as a team?"

Even as she derided the idea, she rather liked it. Her father had always encouraged her to explore the world with open curiosity and with his passing, she felt rather alone. As much as she loved Maisie, they'd never been overly close given her sister had lived with their aunt for many years. Maisie did at least understand her desire for something more than the life of a wife whereas their mother simply stared at Ginny as though she were some strange creature rising from the depths every time she discussed the idea of studying history further.

Of course, there had been a fleeting hope marrying Sir Horace would allow her to be part of a team of two.

Silly her. He'd laughed in her face when she suggested she could aid him in his research.

"Ginny?"

She gave herself a little shake and offered a smile even though Pierce wouldn't be able to see it from behind her.

"My reasons aren't important." After all, she was hardly worth scouring the country for. Sir Horace was probably spending more time searching for his stolen carriage than a missing fiancé.

When Pierce dismounted, she put her fingers in his before she thought too carefully about it. His gloved hand closed in around hers and even with her tatty, borrowed gloves that didn't fit very well, the difference in size sent a strange sensation to the pit of her stomach. She snatched her hand back and dismounted quickly.

Pierce gave her an amused look which she ignored.

"I'm assuming you've been here before," he asked.

She nodded. "Many a time. It's the nearest castle ruin to Oakfield."

Youssef tethered the horses to a nearby tree and they made their way up the steep slope to the ruins.

"Why you English have to build your castles on mountains I do not know," Youssef grumbled, panting.

"It's a hill," Pierce pointed out.

"And an excellent defense against invaders," Ginny added.

"But it's bad for my knees." Youssef paused to take a breath and waved a hand. "Go on without me. My old bones need a rest."

Pierce shook his head. "You're a mere five years older than me."

"Try telling that to my bones, my lord," Youssef replied. "Some of us aren't so lucky to have been raised in grand houses with a cook to bow to my every whim."

Pierce lifted his gaze to the sky and leaned in as he and Ginny continued to make their way up the slope. "Youssef is the son of a wealthy businessman. He hardly grew up in the gutters."

Ginny didn't know how to respond so said nothing. Youssef had been nothing but kind to her and she had to wonder why he was so loyal to a man like Pierce if his livelihood didn't depend on it.

They stopped at the top of the hill and Pierce twisted to glance at the view behind them. Ginny lifted her gaze to eye the crumbling walls of the old castle as she gathered her breath.

Vines crept over the weathered stones and shafts of light pierced through gaps in the canopy overhead, illuminating motes of dust that danced in the damp air.

Pierce ran his hand along a section of wall, tracing the lichen with his fingers. "Cromwell did a fine job pulling this one down."

The huge tower was completely slighted on one side, the evidence of the pulling down of one wall left littered about the mound in the form of giant slabs of stone.

"He did unfortunately." Ginny trailed behind, skimming the vegetation with her eyes. "It dates back to the early medieval period. Can you imagine the history these walls have witnessed?"

"It's quite the castle," Pierce agreed.

"I do not see how this will help us find any clues as to where the treasure went."

"Sometimes it helps to start at the beginning."

She couldn't argue against that. It made sense. But she didn't like agreeing with Pierce either. It was far easier to be at opposite ends of an opinion. Finding common ground with such a man made her uneasy.

Ginny took a step forward and winced, biting back a curse word. She looked to the ground to spy a piece of rusted metal poking out of one of the stones. Her thin trousers offered little protection against the sharp metal, and she felt something damp trickle down her leg.

"Blast." Sparing a glance at Pierce who had made his way into the main keep of the castle, she paused to roll up her trouser leg and explore the graze. It was deeper than expected and the blood didn't stop when she pressed her trousers to it, not to mention the wound stung horribly.

"Hurry up, sweeting." Pierce's voice echoed from somewhere in the castle. "Can't keep up with those short legs?"

Teeth gritted, Ginny rolled down her trouser leg and forced herself to walk as normally as she could. There was no chance she was letting *this* man see her as weak.

∞∞∞

Pierce's footsteps echoed throughout the castle as he explored the ruins. He didn't expect to find any immediate clues as to the whereabouts of the treasure, but he couldn't deny the allure of exploring the ancient castle. A thrill whispered through him when he thought of the last people to defend this castle and the hundreds of lives lived in the crumbling walls.

They reached the remains of what must have been the great hall. The roof had long since collapsed, and the floor was now just a jumbled mess of fallen stones.

Above them, remains of old fireplaces carved into the walls marked each floor. Even with one side of the tall tower missing, it was hard to imagine how such a fortress had ever been taken.

Ginny came up beside him and peered up. "It would have been four stories high, see?" She motioned to the square holes that would have held the flooring joists. "We're in the cellar."

His temptation to give her a sarcastic response dried on his tongue when he glanced at her. Eyes filled with wonder, a slight smile curving her lips, he saw the same feeling he experienced every time he visited somewhere historic on her face. Whether it was a tomb or a Greek temple, he never lost that feeling of reverence when he stepped foot in such places.

"What do you know of the castle's history?" he asked.

"It was originally built in the Norman era." She motioned about them. "This is the oldest part of it."

"Indeed."

"It was added to significantly over the years. I saw some drawings once of the Elizabethan additions." She pointed toward an entrance on the opposite side of the ruin. "They didn't fare as well as the keep, considering the walls were not really built for defense and more for decoration.

He eyed her for a few moments. At least he knew he hadn't been wrong about her. Ginny's knowledge of Oakfield and its history was better than even he realized. Pierce had a strong knowledge of the castle given how often his uncle talked of it, but he'd never dug so deeply into the research surrounding the castle to find floor plans.

"During the civil war it was taken by the Parliamentarians," Pierce said. "Though it never faced a battle after that, but they didn't want to risk it being taken back."

Her small fists balled at her sides. "Such a waste."

"Agreed."

"Presumably your treasure was long gone by then."

He nodded. "The castle was taken in 1642. Sir Richard emptied the building of its wealth the year before."

She huffed out a breath. "I'm not certain how looking around the castle will help."

"Ready to turn around and give up then?" he asked, grinning.

"Never." Her chin rose on cue. "But what can we hope to find that hasn't already been found? Surely you do not expect to find some trail of coins leading to the hoard?"

"No, of course not. But it always helps to start at the beginning."

"How wise of you," she said with a roll of her eyes.

"When you have travelled the world and explored dozens of ancient wonders, perhaps *you* can come up with the plan of action."

"If I had a plan of action, it would not involve looting hidden treasure for my own gain."

"Oh? And what would it involve?"

"Putting it somewhere for all to see. There's a huge museum in London now."

"That's private," he reminded her.

"But you can request entry."

"And how many people do you think request entry?"

"Well..." Her cheeks pinkened. "That's not the point. It shouldn't be bought by some awful wealthy lord or merchant who will hide it away for generations to come."

"Like me, you mean?"

Ginny twisted to eye him. "It's hard to recall you are the heir to a dukedom. You certainly don't look like a duke."

Pierce ran a hand over the stubble on his jaw. Keeping up appearances had never appealed to him much. It all seemed a waste of time when one could be doing much more exciting things.

"Just think yourself lucky I'm not forcing you to address me by my full title."

"Which is?"

"Lord Pierce Elliot, Marquis of Beneford, Earl of Langfield, Viscount Oxhurst."

She blinked a few times then pressed her lips together. "If you expect me to be impressed by that, I'm not."

"So what impresses you, Miss Beaufort?"

"Well, certainly not titles or wealth or...or muscles." She waved a vague hand at him.

"So you've noticed?"

"Noticed what?" The pink in her cheeks darkened. "How you puff out your chest every time a woman is near?" She shook her head. "Do not worry, I have never cared one whit for whether a man has muscles or not. I'm more interested in what is in his mind."

"There's plenty in my mind," he replied. "Just because you can't look past my muscles—"

"I am not distracted by your muscles." She turned away from him and as she stomped off toward the rear door, her leg buckled, and a slight cry escaped her.

Hastening over, Pierce tried to take her arm as she put a hand to the wall.

"I'm fine," she said, snatching her arm back.

He glanced her over, his gaze landing on the leg she couldn't seem to put weight on. "What have you done?" he demanded, dropping to his knees.

Before she could protest, he hiked up her trouser leg, revealing pale, smooth skin.

"Get off," she protested and flapped a hand at him.

"Not a chance." Dry blood stained the hem of her trousers, and he shoved them higher to reveal a gash in her calf, still damp with blood. "Bloody idiot," he muttered. "How did you do this?"

She refused to meet his gaze as he looked up at her. "It's nothing."

"It's deep enough. You'll be lucky if it does not get infected and fall off."

She looked at him then, eyes wide. "It's not that bad."

He issued an irritated sigh and rose. "Sit."

Ginny remained standing.

He affected his most lordly expression. "Sit."

Slowly, reluctantly, she sank onto the crumbling remains of the stone pillar nearby. She folded her arms while Pierce dropped down in front of her once more.

"We should at least bind it."

"Oh yes, with all the bandages I have upon me."

He ignored the remark and shucked off his coat and undid his jacket. Forgoing the wardrobe of a duke had its benefits at times. The thin fabric of his shirt gave way with ease when he pulled at the neckline.

"What on earth are you doing?"

He yanked again, the ripping echoing off the damp walls, and he managed to tear free a strip of fabric.

"But your shirt," she protested.

"Is cheap and inconsequential."

He lifted her boot into his lap and gently laid the fabric over the wound. She hissed.

"Forgive me," he said, then eased the bandage around her calf and cinched it tight. She whimpered slightly while he bound it and regret tugged at his insides. The woman might be a pain in his rear, but he didn't wish harm on her.

Pierce eased down her trouser leg and looked up at her. "You should ensure you clean that thoroughly when you get home. And don't ever do that again."

"Hurt myself?"

"Keep an injury a secret." He rose to standing. "We're a team and we look out for one another."

"Even if we don't like each other?"

"Even then."

She opened her mouth to say something, but Youssef stepped into the room, his rasping breaths bounding off the walls.

"Oh there you are!" He glanced between them, his gaze landing upon Pierce's torn shirt. "Seriously, Pierce, I cannot leave you alone for a moment."

Ginny opened her mouth to protest but Pierce held up a hand. "Don't bother," he said. "Youssef is immature for his age and cannot resist teasing whenever he has the chance."

His friend smirked but Pierce couldn't help but be glad the man had interrupted their conversation. For some reason, Ginny was becoming a distraction he didn't need, and he had a task to complete.

Chapter Seven

It was a fine job her sister didn't depend on Ginny's aid at the inn because her leg was making her entirely useless. At least it wasn't infected Ginny supposed. She'd so hate to have proven Pierce right and she could almost imagine his smug impression were she struck down with illness.

Hobbling around upstairs, however, also meant she couldn't accompany Pierce and Youssef on their trip to the village near Heversham Castle. Their hope was to talk to some members of the village in case any of their ancestors had passed down tales of the castle.

She sighed and rested against the doorway of the empty guest bedroom for a moment. She would have loved to have been there to hear any stories they dug up.

Ginny entered the room and closed the door before she began to strip the bed sheets. If she couldn't help downstairs, she refused to sit around and sulk about missing out on the treasure hunt.

After piling up the bedding, she walked around the bed to clear up a tankard and newspaper that had been left on the dressing table. A glance at the headline had her heart stuttering.

She picked up the newspaper, her pulse surging through her body. "He's here."

The paper shook in her hands as she skimmed the article alongside an illustration of a carriage.

The very carriage she stole from Sir Horace.

Ginny set the paper down and took in a long, unsteady

breath. She knew he'd probably track down the carriage, though she'd rather imagined Sir Horace would send people to do it for him. It seemed he found the carriage where she left it, and the article described the man's hunt for his stolen vehicle.

What it didn't say was whether he had returned to Scotland. It didn't mention her either, though she had little idea if he had figured out she took it. The man made it clear he thought little of women entirely and being so bold was not exactly in her nature.

Ginny usually considered every decision in great detail. It was precisely why she agreed to marry the man. She'd pictured their life together quite carefully, knowing she could fulfill the role of a wife if needs be, so long as it gave her access to Sir Horace's research. After all, no women could be a historian but being a historian's wife was almost as good.

"He'll have gone home," she told herself.

She'd seen the disappointment when he'd set eyes on her. No doubt Mother sent him the tiny cameo painting, the one that had been done before her cheeks filled out, that barely looked like her at all.

Ginny snatched up the newspaper and rolled it up to shove under her arm. "He'll have gone home," she repeated.

The carriage theft was only written about because nothing remarkable ever happened in Rothbury and a carriage was more valuable to Sir Horace than an errant wife-to-be who was plain and boring.

A tap at the door made her heart jolt into her throat. She relaxed when Maisie put her head around the door. "Betty said you were up here."

Ginny gestured to the stripped bed. "Just trying to make myself useful."

Maisie gave her a doubtful look. "So long as you do not injure yourself further."

"My leg is perfectly fine, just a little sore."

"Well, I found the books you requested. I spoke to Lord Blackthorpe and, thankfully, they have a well-stocked library. He gave me a few books, but he promised to have any others he finds sent over."

"Did you request any about the civil war?"

Maisie nodded. "Of course."

"Sorry, I do not mean to be ungrateful." She puffed out a breath.

Maisie didn't deserve Ginny being short with her, no matter how terrified she was about being discovered. Her sister had aided her against her better judgement and was still helping her now.

Her sister tilted her head. "Oh, Ginny, I didn't think you were being ungrateful."

"Still, I should be thanking you for doing that for me. And Lord Blackthorpe. Maybe once I'm no longer in hiding I can visit him and thank him in person."

Maisie thrust a thumb behind her. "I left the books in your room but I'm not sure what you hope to discover."

"I doubt Pierce has bothered to read any books about the local history," Ginny said. "Maybe I'll discover something he doesn't know."

"If you do not like the man, I don't understand why you are helping him."

"Well, if he discovers any treasure, perhaps I can persuade him to be respectful of it and ensure it is displayed somewhere for everyone to appreciate."

Her sister gave her an amused look. "I still remember you digging around in the dirt as a little girl hoping you would find something valuable."

"I did find an old roman coin once," Ginny reminded her.

"It's true. And after that not even Papa could drag you away from that field."

Ginny chuckled at the memory and then sighed. "I just want to be a part of something, you know? Something that matters."

"You do matter, Ginny. To me and to Apollo."

She noticed Maisie didn't mention the rest of her family, though. She doubted her mother and other siblings cared that much about where she'd gone. Gone were the days of being humble innkeepers in the village they all loved.

Once their brother started to earn a fine living as a lawyer, her entire family seemed to change. All they spoke of was impressing the nobility and ensuring they continued their rise through society. It had been made clear Ginny's only value was to find a suitable husband who could continue to ensure the Beauforts made their mark on London. Everyone had been astonished and far too grateful that Ginny had accepted the offer of the famous Sir Horace Robertson.

"Why don't you go and sit down for a while and peruse those books?" her sister suggested.

Ginny shook her head. "I should help you."

"I hate to say it, Ginny, but Betty can strip those beds in half the time you can while you're hobbling around on that injured leg."

"And I'm getting in the way," Ginny said for her.

A common occurrence for her given she had no beauty and no skills to make her remarkable enough to be of use to people.

"Ginny..."

"It's fine," she assured her sister. "I'm looking forward to digging through those books.

She stopped in front of her sister and gave her a slightly awkward embrace. At least if anything came out of this disaster, her relationship with Maisie would be much improved.

∞∞∞

The scurry of movement as soon as Pierce entered the house made his lips curve. He handed over his hat and coat to the butler, ignoring the disapproving look from the man and the slight rattle of a vase upon a table as someone very small tried to remain out of sight.

When he took a few steps forward, she leapt out from her hiding spot and jumped in front of him, hands raised like the claws of a wild animal. He laughed and pressed a hand to his chest. His little sister didn't need to pretend to be a wild animal. From her frizzy hair that could never be tamed, to the way her skirts always seemed to be streaked with mud, she was about as wild as they came. He eyed the ten-year-old who crossed her arms and pouted. All of his siblings shared the same golden hair, but Hester looked and behaved most like him.

"Why can I never, ever scare you?" she asked.

"Because I am always ready."

She unfolded her arms and wagged a finger at him. "One day, I'll get you."

He grinned. "I have no doubt about it."

"Did you bring anything for me?" she asked coyly.

He thrust a hand into his pocket and pulled out a brown bag of sherbet lemons, pausing a moment before handing them over. "Have you been good for Mama?"

His sister looked briefly at the ornate ceiling above. "Define good."

"Helpful then."

"Well, I only got a little muddy today, and I did spend some time doing some cross-stitching, though I'm never any good at it. Everything I make looks ugly."

"I'm sure that's not true."

Hester eyed him boldly. "I'm not silly, you know. I'm well aware of what is ugly and what is not."

"Very well then. I'm sure it was exceedingly ugly."

She nodded firmly. "Exceedingly." She glanced about the empty hallway. "But I've been keeping out of Mama's way when she needs me to."

Pierce's heart sank a little. Hester wasn't a troublesome girl, not really. She just wasn't interested in typical female hobbies, and he blamed himself for that in many ways. He hadn't been around enough, and she'd taken to mimicking his adventures by way of running around in the gardens or getting lost for hours in the coppice at the edge of the estate.

He handed over the packet of sherbets and she dug straight in, stuffing two in her mouth.

"You know," she said, her voice muffled by the sweets. "When Giles said you were coming home, I thought we would see more of you."

"I'm sorry, Hettie. I will be around more once I've found this treasure."

Her eyes gleamed at the mention of treasure. "Have you made any progress?"

"None yet." Pierce rubbed a hand across his rough jaw. "But we do have someone to speak to who might know something about its whereabouts."

"I always thought finding treasure was just about digging in the ground, but you haven't done any digging yet."

"Maybe I won't have to. Lots of treasures are found above ground—it's just very hidden."

"Pierce," she said seriously, "when you find it, will you show me?"

"Of course I will."

If he ever found it, that was. He kept finding his usual optimism waning. Perhaps it was because his uncle had spent his whole life hoping to find it or maybe it was because of the urgency of the matter. All of this, from Hettie's grubby expensive gowns to the paintings that hung in the hallway for over a hundred years, could be lost if he didn't find the treasure, and all because he had been away, indulging his whims while his family suffered.

"Ah, Pierce." His father appeared in the doorway of the study, slightly disheveled but his cheeks full of warmth and his eyes unusually bright. "I thought I heard your voice. Care to join me in my study for a moment?"

Pierce shared a look with his sister who shrugged and dashed off upstairs, probably intending to eat all the sherbets in one go before she could be stopped.

"How are you feeling, Father?" Pierce asked as he followed the Duke of Marbury into the study.

"Oh quite well, quite well."

The once neat study was a mess of letters, books, and open

ledgers. Pierce gestured to the accounts book. "You know this is Mr. Ledbury's job."

His father shut the door, peering up at him through wire-rimmed spectacles. "I fear he hasn't been doing his job very well. Things seem in disarray." He motioned to the pile of unopened letters. "And it seems I've not been getting my post on time." He picked a letter up and waved it at him. "Look, this is from three weeks ago."

"Well, the roads aren't very good at the moment," Pierce said feebly.

His father's lucid moments were so few and far between, the last thing he wanted to do was ruin this one and explain to him the letters arrived well on time and had been piling up while his father had been abed or wandering about the house in a daze.

He considered the stack of letters then looked at his father. Physically strong with a thick head of sandy white hair, it seemed so wrong that such a man would be brought low by an addled mind.

"I'll help you with the correspondence," Pierce offered.

"Don't you have somewhere to be?"

He was meant to meet Youssef at the inn, but it could wait. The person they wished to speak to could wait and Youssef wouldn't mind spending the day drinking ale and eating pies.

"Not at all, but I just need to send a quick message."

His father gave him a grateful smile that made his gut twist. He should have been here. For all of them.

After finding the butler and dispatching a message to Youssef, he came upon the majority of his siblings in the east parlor room, arguing over whether Byron was really an attractive man or not.

"It's the clothes that make him," said Rebecca, and Pierce found himself slightly grateful the sixteen-year-old didn't care for Byron. Perhaps they would be safe from her making any unseemly decisions when it came to men anytime soon.

"Nonsense." Jules folded her arms. "He could wear a sackcloth and still be a fine-looking man."

"I do think it's all become a little ridiculous," said Peter. "Who cares how he styles his hair or wears his cravat?"

"You," retorted Jules. "I saw you trying to style your hair just like his."

Vincent rolled his eyes, his arm resting upon the mantlepiece. "Am I really meant to spend five hours a day trying to look like that?"

Rebecca shook her head. "No, that's Brummel."

Vincent peered at her. "What's Brummel got to do with Byron?"

"He's the one who says you should spend endless hours a day getting dressed," explained Rebecca.

Vincent glanced Pierce's way and gave him a relieved look as the argument swayed toward how much time one should devote to one's outer appearance. Given Pierce didn't think much about it at all, he didn't think he had anything useful to say.

Vincent headed over to join Pierce in the doorway. "I'm glad you're here to save me from this madness." His brother's expression darkened. "Poor choice of words."

"How has Father been?"

"Quite well since yesterday. But before that, pretty terrible."

"I'm going to aid him with some correspondence in just a moment. He seemed hale."

Vincent sighed. "He has good and bad days. I'm trying to help where I can but for all her trying to be brave, Mother is struggling."

Pierce nodded. "Her husband of nearly forty years is losing his mind. It's not surprising." He eased out a breath. "I should have been here sooner, Vincent. This shouldn't have all been on you and Mother."

His eldest brother clapped a hand to his shoulder and gave him a strained smile. "You're here now, that's all that matters. With any luck, between us we'll ensure the family is protected."

Pierce swallowed hard. He had a sinking feeling that it was too late for that. The duke's mind was slipping away, and with it, their family's wealth and reputation. But he couldn't dwell on that now, not when the treasure offered them a chance to save everything, and he would do just that.

Chapter Eight

Ginny stretched her arm up, nearly touching the shelf with the tips of her fingers. The teapot grazed against them, and she let out an exasperated groan. Determinedly, she tried to reach higher once more.

"You can tell these shelves were designed by a man," she said as she strained to somehow grow taller.

"Or by a normal-sized person."

She tossed a scowl over her shoulder. Pierce leaned against the doorframe of the kitchen as though he owned the inn, a wry smile of amusement pulled across a cleanly shaven jaw.

I miss the beard.

She batted the thought away. She didn't care if he was covered from head to toe in hair.

"I'm average height," she protested.

"If average means small, then yes, you are definitely average height."

He entered the kitchen as she moved onto tiptoes once more. If she could just—

The world fell from beneath her feet as hands clamped around her waist and she found herself floating upwards toward the shelf.

"What are you…" she spluttered. "You can't just…"

"Just get the teapot."

She snatched and held it close while Pierce lowered her to the floor with ease. Whirling, she glared at him.

"You cannot just handle me as though I am

some...some...damsel in distress."

"You're hardly damsel material, sweeting." Amusement glinted in his eyes.

God, she hated how he always seemed to be laughing at her. She knew it was ridiculous and entirely illogical running around hunting treasure and dressing as a boy, but he had no idea how serious her situation was. If Sir Horace found her, she'd be forced into a marriage with a monster of a man. Her fiancé had made it very clear she would have no chance of breaking it off without ruination.

Ginny set the teapot on the side. "You could have simply grabbed the pot for me," she snapped.

"Where is the fun in that?" Pierce took a step back, the sun streaming in through the windows glinting on his hair and highlighting what looked to be slight shadows under his eyes.

The dark circles almost set her off kilter. What could possibly affect this man's sleep? She'd wager her freedom on him sleeping like a newborn with nothing more to worry about than where his next adventure would be.

"I'm not here for your amusement," she told him.

"You know, for such a small package, you hold an awful lot of anger."

"I would imagine you would not be too happy to be dismissed simply because of your size or sex but I do not suppose you can sympathize with such a thing." She pressed her lips together and eyed him. "In fact, I'm not certain you are capable of sympathy at all."

Something flickered briefly in his eyes as though she had struck him somewhere deep but that couldn't be possible. A man like Pierce had an ego that was entirely impenetrable. No doubt he'd been told he was the cleverest and strongest and most handsome man in the world since birth.

"Think positively," he quipped. "At least you're closer to the sink."

The half-hearted quip didn't strike nearly as deep as he might have intended, even as Ginny tried to remain annoyed at him. She recognized the statement for what it was—some form of defense.

"Insulting my height *and* my sex? That's a new low for you, my lord."

He lifted a shoulder. "I try."

"I'm assuming you came here to tell me something and not just to insult me."

"Do you know a Mary Bradford? She resides in Oakfield."

"Mary Bradford?" Ginny repeated, leaning back against the kitchen counter. "I don't think so."

"She's meant to have lived here for some time."

"Oh, maybe that's Misty Mary. I've never even heard her surname uttered." She shook her head. "Anyone who lives here long enough winds up with a nickname. There are some people whose real name I don't even know."

"Do you have a nickname?"

"Why would I have a nickname? No one knows I'm here."

"But I have it on good authority the Beauforts have run this inn for over twenty years."

Her heart gave a little skip and she forced herself to keep her expression placid as he inched closer.

What else did he know of her? What would he do when he found out she was running from a fiancé?

She curled her hands around the countertop and dug her fingernails into the wood.

"I'll admit, Ginny, I fail to see why you should wish to be in disguise around people you've known all your life."

"As I have said before, it's personal."

His gaze searched hers and the scent of cologne reached her. She didn't know what he'd been doing the past two days but apparently a lot of it had involved shaving and dousing himself in something other than soap and water.

The expensive fragrance clinging to him didn't seem to fit with the haphazard way his hair was styled or the open collar. She suspected she preferred the soap smell.

Ginny held his gaze firmly and he stepped back and lifted his palms. "Fine, don't tell me, but if you are some murderer on the run, I had better not be arrested for aiding you."

"Do I look like a murderer?"

He glanced her up and down. "I'd never underestimate you, Ginny Beaufort."

For some reason, the compliment warmed her. No one expected anything from plain Ginny. She wondered if that was why Sir Horace had chosen her. Plain boring Ginny wouldn't expect anything from a husband surely?

She swallowed past the slight knot in her throat and shoved away from the side, putting the kitchen table between her and Pierce.

"I know where Mary lives. What do you want with her?"

"According to the people we spoke with, her family used to reside near Heversham Castle, and were known to have been around at the time of the civil war. There's a high chance one of her family members worked in the castle."

"Well, I can take you there," she offered, "but I'm not certain how much sense we can get from her. Misty Mary can be a little…" Ginny paused and tried to summon kindly way of saying it "…obtuse."

"I'm sure I can persuade her to tell us something of use."

Ginny shook her head and patted his arm. "I'm sure you can, Pierce. I'm sure you can."

∞∞∞∞

"Should you be accompanying us, Ginny?" Youssef asked. "Your leg is still healing surely?"

Pierce forced himself to cease glaring at Youssef's back. A day of drinking and eating at the inn had brightened his friend's spirits and, for some reason, he was more charming than ever. Why Pierce should mind that charm being used on Ginny, he did not know. After all, the more charmed she was, the more likely it was that she'd help them, and she had proven to be of aid once more, directing them to Mary's small cottage.

"My leg is only a little sore now," Ginny told Youssef cheerfully. "And I can't stand being forced to remain abed."

Pierce ground his teeth together. He hadn't even considered asking about her leg. He'd just assumed as she was working in the kitchen that all was well.

Ginny might think him an arrogant arse, but he hadn't intended on sealing that reputation so firmly. He'd have to do better. Be nicer. More charming.

Youssef gave her a little nudge with his elbow as he and Ginny walked side by side down the country lane. "Well, you look remarkably well considering."

Letting his scowl deepen, Pierce stared at the back of his friend's head as though he could transmit his thoughts to him. *Cease being so damned pleasant to her.* Youssef was making Pierce look bad. Of course he noticed her cheeks were quite pink now and the wintery sunlight flattered her green eyes, but he damn well wasn't going to start spouting about it.

"Here's Mary's house." She gestured toward the cottage at the end of the lane.

Flowers and herbs flourished in the front garden, almost hiding the building from view. Ivy crawled up the brick walls and clung to window frames that looked so old it seemed a breeze might turn them to dust. It was strange to think the key to finding the treasure might be living in this odd little building.

Ginny led the way, knocking five times, in a very specific pattern. Pierce lifted his brows and Ginny gave him a resigned look.

"If someone doesn't know Mary's 'knock' she seldom bothers to answer the door," Ginny explained.

"A fine job we have you here then," Youssef said.

"I was going to say just that," Pierce muttered.

Youssef frowned at Pierce. "What's wrong with you today? You're acting like a bear with a sore head."

"Nothing," Pierce grumbled, but he knew it was a lie. It was Ginny causing this. She was getting under his skin for some reason, and he didn't like it one bit.

The door creaked open, revealing a small, elderly woman with a cloud of white hair around her head and a sharp, birdlike appearance.

"Mary...I mean Miss Bradford," Ginny said. "I was hoping you could spare some time. These gentlemen are here to ask you a few questions."

Mary's eyes narrowed and she stared at Ginny for some time. "How did you know my knock?"

"Uh..." Ginny's face flushed. They'd all forgotten Ginny's disguise.

The woman inclined her head then looked at Pierce and Youssef. "Questions? What kind of questions?"

"About your family in Heversham," Youssef said politely.

Mary looked Youssef up and down and a wicked grin split across her face. "I sense something special in you, young man." She grabbed his arm.

Youssef chuckled. "She thinks I'm a young man, Pierce," he managed to say before Mary dragged him into the house.

"She must be blind."

Ginny swung a glance his way. "Youssef is right. You really are quite grumpy today."

It hadn't started this way. Spending the day aiding his father had left him feeling quite positive. Perhaps things weren't as bad as they all feared. The whole family sat down and eaten dinner together just like old times and his father had been back to his normal self. He still needed the treasure to make up for the mismanagement that had taken place when his father's mental state began to decline, but if they could have more days like yesterday...

"Are you coming?" Ginny gestured impatiently from inside the narrow, dark hallway of the cottage.

He ducked inside and followed Ginny into a tiny parlor room that smelled of pine needles and sage. Knitted blankets covered every chair in a variety of colors and Youssef had been seated in pride of place near the fireplace as though he was a king holding court.

"Can I get you some tea?" Miss Bradford asked. "And some cake perhaps."

"Tea and cake would be most excellent." Youssef ignored Pierce's bemused look.

The man sat straighter and spoke more politely than Pierce had ever witnessed, and they had been invited to dine with many a royal family during their adventures.

The woman hastened out of the room as Pierce and Ginny sat and a clatter and some faint humming could be heard while they waited. Finally, she emerged with a tray of mismatched cups and a slab of some sort of plain cake that sagged in the middle.

"I find it important to maintain one's balance with the world," Miss Bradford said as she set the tray on the table in the middle of the room. "So I do not keep cow's milk or use eggs in my cakes, but I think you'll quite enjoy this replacement milk." She gestured to the dainty milk jug. "I squeeze the milk from oats, and you can scarcely tell the difference." She poured the tea and handed Youssef a cup first. "And, of course, I do not need to worry about keeping it cool."

"You are quite industrious, Miss Bradford."

"Oh you must call me Mary, Youssef," she said, and Pierce wondered if she was going to bother asking him and Ginny for their names.

"This looks wonderful, Mary." Youssef took a sip of Mary's tea, only to put the cup and saucer down sharply. "A little hot," he commented hoarsely and made a furtive gesture for Pierce and Ginny not to drink it.

"So" —Mary seated herself next to Youssef and carved the cake— "what did you fine men wish to ask of me?"

"You're family used to reside in Heversham, did they not?" Pierce asked.

"Oh yes, for centuries." Mary smiled wistfully. "My mother moved here to escape, well, some rather unfair rumors."

"People thought she was a witch," Ginny whispered in

Pierce's ear.

"Do you know much of your family's history?" Pierce continued. "Someone suggested they would have worked at Heversham Castle in the past."

"Oh, yes you're right. Most people worked in the castle at one point or another. It's how the village came to be."

Pierce leaned forward, elbows resting on his knees while he cradled the teacup in both hands. "And were any of your ancestors working there around the time the castle was pulled down?"

Mary wrinkled her nose. "I should think so. The castle was one of the only ways of making a living until it was pulled down." She shifted forward in her chair and sliced up the cake, carefully setting each slice on plates before handing them out.

Pierce took a bite without thinking and coughed. He'd had mouthfuls of sand that tasted better. Somehow, he choked down his bite and pushed on.

"So they did work there? Do you know anything about what happened prior to its occupation by the Parliamentarians?" Pierce pressed.

Mary's eyes glazed over slightly. "*I thought of Thee, my partner and my guide,*

As being past away.—Vain sympathies!

For, backward, Duddon! as I cast my eyes," she paused and frowned then started the poem again with renewed gusto. "*And if, as toward the silent tomb we go, Through love, through hope, and faith's transcendent dower, We feel that we are greater than we know.*"

"What is that from, Mary?" asked Ginny.

"Oh you're a smart girl. I'm sure you'll help these gentlemen find whatever it is they are seeking."

Ginny's mouth dropped open and Mary urged the plate of cake toward her. "Eat up, dear. It seems to me you'll need your strength and determination in the coming days."

Pierce resisted the desire to pinch the bridge of his nose. The rate this hunt was going, they'd all need a lot more than dry cake to keep up their strength and determination.

Chapter Nine

"You do not seem worried Mary has figured out who you are," Pierce murmured to Ginny as they ducked out of the cottage.

Ginny glanced back at the building. Of all the people to discover her, she never thought it would be Mary. She'd been 'obtuse' for as long as Ginny remembered.

"I don't think she'll tell anyone and if she did, no one would believe her. She's known for her fanciful tales."

"And fanciful poems," Youssef added.

"Anyone know what poem that was?" Pierce asked.

She shook her head. "I've never been one for poetry."

"Nor me." Pierce shrugged. "Much to my father's annoyance."

They started their journey back to the village, side by side with Ginny between the two men. Both men had somehow maneuvered her between them like they wanted to protect her from anyone they might meet on the road. Walking between two strong men was rather wasted on her, she feared, and her sisters would likely take much more pleasure in it, but it wasn't an entirely horrible experience either.

She glanced at Pierce. "Your father likes poetry?"

"I'll ask him if he knows it, though whether he is—" Pierce paused. "He might not remember."

Youssef shrugged. "I know nothing of English poetry. Always seemed a little depressing to me."

"I doubt it's relevant, but I think we should look into it, do you not think, Ginny?"

Ginny forced herself not to reveal the surprise that Pierce had asked the question of her. No man apart from her father ever cared for her opinion. She narrowed her gaze at him. Perhaps he was teasing.

He gave her a slightly puzzled look. "You *do* think it means something?"

"Oh." She shook her head vigorously. He *had* been serious. "Knowing Mary, probably not, I'm afraid, but it wouldn't hurt to find out what poem it is, just in case it's a clue."

"Damn," Pierce muttered.

"Anyone want cake?" Youssef unfolded the small brown parcel Mary handed him as they left.

Ginny took a small piece and shoved it in her mouth, the dry texture competing with the sweet, spicy flavor of the sponge.

Youssef's dark brows lifted. "Do not tell me you like it?"

Ginny raised her palms. "It reminds me of my childhood. Mary was always quite generous with her cakes, even when people were content to do without."

"When did you leave Oakfield?" Youssef said.

"Quite a few years ago now." She glanced between the two men, uncertain how much she should reveal. London was vast and filled with people and she was used to going unnoticed, but it didn't seem wise to give the man blackmailing her any additional information.

"Give me a small village over a busy town any day," Youssef commented.

She didn't disagree, however, she never resented leaving Oakfield as much as Maisie did. After all, following her brother to London seemed logical. It would give her sisters a chance to find good husbands who could look after them and Mother never really enjoyed the life of an innkeeper's wife.

"So what next?" Ginny asked.

"We continue our search," Pierce replied. "We read every book we can find and trace anyone else along the road from the castle who might have had ancestors here." He removed his hat, scraped his hand through his hair, and put it back on. "I can request records for the local area from Parliament, though they'll take a while to arrive."

"Some of the churches will have old records of marriages," Ginny commented. "Perhaps some that date back to the civil war."

Pierce smiled at her, the curve of his lips making her stomach feel slightly odd and heavy. "A fine idea. They often list occupations too."

"I'll continue making some inquiries among the locals," Youssef chimed in.

"And what about the poem?" She asked. "Should we look into that as well?"

Pierce stared ahead for a moment before nodding. "It may be nothing, but it's worth investigating."

"You said the sketch—"

"Map," Pierce corrected.

"The sketch," she continued, "was your uncle's. Surely he has records of his search for the treasure? Would it not make sense not to start from there?"

Pierce gave a tight smile. "My uncle died in Italy, and we've yet to have all his belongings returned to us." His expression turned troubled. "He was never the most organized of men either."

"Did he leave something at your father's house perhaps? We could go search—"

"No," Pierce snapped, his tone so cold she almost leapt back a pace. "There's nothing there."

She stared at him. "Well, there's no need—"

"It's not happening, Ginny." Pierce stomped ahead briskly, and she watched his agitated movements for a moment before looking at Youssef, who eyed his friend with concern.

"What was that about?" she whispered.

"He's under a great deal of strain at the moment."

"If this treasure hunt is causing him so much concern, he should give it up."

Though she had to admit, the last thing she wanted to do was stop now. They might not have found out anything more but...

"He can't," Youssef confided. "He needs this more than you know."

She watched as Pierce plucked a brown leaf from a low-hanging branch and tossed it to the side. She shouldn't want to know. After all, he'd done nothing but tease her and cause her aggravation, yet she couldn't silence the curious voice that had her wishing to understand this adventuring nobleman.

∞∞∞

Feeling no better than a sulky child, Pierce stomped on. He didn't owe her an apology or an explanation. Not really. He didn't owe Ginny anything. If she wanted to keep her secrets, he could keep his and the last thing anyone needed to know was that the Duke of Marbury was losing his mind.

Yet the sinking feeling in his stomach told him otherwise. He paused by a small wooden bridge that crossed the river that came from Oakfield. He heard Ginny and Youssef's voices above the rush of water, but they trailed behind him, apparently quite content to talk of Youssef's childhood in Egypt and how he had come to work with Pierce.

Pierce leaned against the railing and eyed the bubbling water. He was being ridiculous, and he knew it. But all he could picture was his siblings arguing in the parlor room. His family could find any number of minor things to disagree about, but they were as close as they came. If their financial situation did not improve swiftly, they'd have to let the house, sell off much-loved belongings and likely all be tossed to the wind. His sisters would have to marry quickly, and his brothers would have to find work outside of the estate.

But what if they never found anything? What if it was all for naught? He couldn't bear the thought of failure, not when so much was riding on this. He needed to keep his head on straight and push aside any distraction, including Ginny.

From the bridge, he noticed a cluster of pink soapworts and grabbed a handful. Ginny didn't deserve him snapping at her.

He waited for Ginny and Youssef to catch up with him, holding the small bouquet of pink flowers. As they approached, Ginny looked up at him, her expression guarded.

"I'm sorry," Pierce said, holding out the flowers. "I didn't mean to snap."

Ginny took the flowers warily as though she'd never been handed flowers before in her life. He didn't know why but he had the sudden desire to give her a giant bouquet of the most expensive flowers one could possibly find.

Behind her, Youssef smirked slightly, and Pierce eyed his friend, silently daring him to make some sarcastic remark.

"They're very lovely," she said softly, and he almost forgot she wore the ugly cap and boy's clothes that fit her so poorly it was no wonder no one had looked twice at her. "But may I remind you, you're blackmailing me into assisting you? By all rights, you could snap at me as much as you wish, and I still have to help."

"You really think I'm still blackmailing you?"

Her eyes widened. "Are you not?"

Pierce gave a lopsided grin. "I know you'd prefer to deny it, but you're as invested in finding this treasure as I am now, Ginny."

"Well, I..." She blew out her cheeks. "That is to say..." Her chin lifted. "I only want to make certain you do the right thing."

"And by the right thing, you mean sell it for an obscene price, right?"

Any softness left her gaze and she glared at him, the flowers clutched in a slowly tightening grip.

That was better. He preferred it this way. Ginny spitting fire at him felt much more normal than whatever it was that had just occurred between them.

Youssef clapped Pierce on the back. "Now that that's settled, shall we continue our search?"

"The church," Pierce announced. "Any chance it's nearby?"

"Yes." Ginny pointed down the road. "It's not far from the village."

"Let's see if we cannot find anything in the marriage records," Pierce said. "Perhaps someone else came from Heversham that we don't know about."

"Sounds good to me," Ginny agreed.

Pierce swung her a sideways glance. "Not worried the vicar might recognize you then."

"I moved out of Oakfield years ago," she explained. "The vicar hasn't seen me since I was a child."

They walked in silence for a while, the sound of their footsteps echoing against the narrow road. The dense foliage of the countryside surrounded them, providing a comforting sense of isolation and privacy. Pierce couldn't help but feel a growing curiosity about Ginny's past and the secrets she held so tightly. There was a vulnerability in her eyes whenever he probed too deeply, as if she was guarding something precious and fragile.

As they approached the village, the sight of the quaint stone church came into view and he went through the ancient wooden gate, past several headstones laid with fresh flowers, and pushed open the creaky doors, revealing an interior bathed in warm sunlight that filtered through the colorful stained-glass windows.

The air was thick with mustiness, as if it had been left undisturbed for years. Rows of pews lined either side of the aisle. At the very front pew, two bonneted heads swiveled their way. One of the young ladies gasped and the other leapt to her feet.

"Lord Beneford!" One of them hastened down the aisle toward him whilst the other snatched a bible and followed her friend.

He studied them both, not recognizing either of them.

He tipped his hat and they tittered. "Ladies."

"We've read all about you." The bible-clutcher smiled, revealing even teeth in amongst a delicate mouth. The rest of her features were similarly petite, contrasting with her friend's more obviously beautiful looks.

Beside him, he felt Ginny stiffen. He was well used to being approached by women, however, he wasn't sure he needed his reputation anymore firmly sealed in her eyes right now.

Pierce glanced at Ginny, who was wearing a guarded expression. He could almost see the thoughts churning through her mind as her chin moved into a determined position. It shouldn't bother him what she thought of him—hell, he never usually cared what people thought—but he was no philanderer and not nearly as much of a rake as the gossip columns painted him as.

He turned his attention back to the two ladies who stood before him with hopeful gazes. The taller one spoke again, her voice tinged with excitement. "We've been following your exploits, my lord. Your quest to find the lost treasure has captured our imaginations."

The shorter girl timidly added, "We simply had to come and see for ourselves. It's all so romantic, don't you think?"

As the girl continued to gush about his exploits, Pierce glanced around the church, searching for any sign of the vicar.

"I'm terribly sorry to interrupt," he interjected smoothly. "We were actually hoping to find the church records. I'm researching some, uh, family history, you see."

"Oh." The taller girl glanced at the floor. "Not looking for treasure then?"

"In Oakfield?" Ginny scoffed. "Hardly likely."

The two girls exchanged looks. "Well, we had better leave you to it," said the lady with the bible. "We're staying at the Bluebell Inn. Perhaps you know it?"

"Actually, I do."

"Perhaps you can regale us with your more exciting tales when you do not have so much company." She swung a pointed look at Ginny before they both dipped and bid him good day.

"Does that happen everywhere you go?" Ginny asked Youssef once the door closed behind the women.

"Everywhere," Youssef said.

"It's to be expected," Pierce replied, rather more primly than he intended. "People always seem to be drawn to the allure of adventure and riches."

Ginny crossed her arms over her chest. "Well, I hope you're not planning on getting distracted by any more admirers. We have a job to do, remember?"

Pierce raised an eyebrow at her, unable to hide his amusement. "Are you jealous, Ginny?"

"Never." Her chin lifted further. "I am not jealous. I just don't like unnecessary distractions, that's all, so let's see if the vicar is in the vestry before anymore admirers turn up."

Pierce chuckled to himself as she stomped off toward the rear of the church. He had to admit, he rather liked the idea of this funny little woman being jealous, though he couldn't quite figure out why.

Chapter Ten

"The door is two steps ahead of you, slightly to the right."

Ginny scowled at Pierce over the stack of books in her arms. They weighed a ton and, admittedly, she couldn't see much over them.

"You could be a gentleman and offer to help." She grunted and shifted the books slightly. "After all, I'm only doing this for you."

Pierce stepped around her, opened the door to her room, and gave a flourishing bow. "My lady."

"That's not the sort of help I meant," she muttered, stepping swiftly past him, and depositing the books onto the edge of the wash stand. The private dining room was occupied, and she couldn't very well dominate the kitchen with a ton of books on such a busy day.

Guilt pricked at her. Here she was, digging through books about poetry and history whilst her sister was earning an independent living. But Maisie insisted she wasn't needed and, if Ginny was honest with herself, she suspected most of the time she just got in the way. Dealing with demanding patrons was not exactly a skill of hers.

"Where's Youssef?" she asked, dropping onto the edge of the bed.

Pierce closed the door to her bedroom and her breath trapped in her throat. He dominated the small room, his head nearly touching the beams above. When he shucked off his greatcoat and slung it over the back of the only chair in the room, revealing his usual cravatless state, she forced herself to take a deep breath.

Ginny glanced at the delicate comb on the table next to the bed and the small, beaded reticule beside it. She'd left in such a rush they were her only belongings in the world at present. Even her clothes had been abandoned since switching with a servant after running from Sir Horace.

Then she looked back at Pierce. Never mind that it would be scandalous to be in a room alone with him if she were back in London, there was something oddly intimate about having him here in her personal space.

"Youssef's happier dashing all over the country, questioning people than digging through books." He dragged the chair across the room and placed it firmly in front of her then sat, lacing his hands behind his head and leaning back. "You're the book expert. Where do you suggest we start?"

"I rather thought you would prefer dashing about the country too," she said, dragging her gaze from the way his arms flexed against his jacket.

The last thing she needed was him thinking she was admiring him in some way. It wasn't that at all. In the narrow confines of her bedroom, he simply occupied a lot of space, and, really, it was hard to look anywhere else.

"And how do you know I'm a book expert?"

"A hunch."

"A hunch?"

He unlaced his hands and lowered them. "My hunches are never wrong."

"You do not go through life simply following your every hunch, surely?"

He shrugged. "I don't know what to say, sweeting. They never fail me. And I have a hunch that you're the only one who can help me find what we're looking for."

Ginny raised an eyebrow. "Is that so? And what makes you think that?"

Pierce leaned forward, the air charged with the intensity of his gaze. "Because you're a puzzle, sweeting. A mystery. And I have a hunch that if anyone can solve it, it's you."

Her heart skipped a beat. He looked at her like he knew something, like he saw more than just a girl in boy's clothing. She tried to swallow past the lump in her throat.

"I'm just a girl who likes books," she said, trying to sound nonchalant.

Pierce leaned back in his chair, a smug grin playing at the corners of his mouth. "And I'm just a man looking for treasure. But somehow, I think we both know that's not the whole truth, now is it?"

"I have no idea what you mean." She rose from the bed and handed him the book at the top of the stack.

"Modern poetry?"

"We have to check every lead, correct?"

"You said Mary often spouts poetry."

Ginny nodded. "And they're often of her own creation, but I do not think we should ignore it either. Mary's method of communication is not always...linear...shall we say? She could have been trying to tell us something."

"Or she's a crazy old lady."

"Mary is many things, but she's not actually mad."

Pierce's gaze grew troubled, and he cleared his throat, and flicked open the book. "Poetry," he murmured. "Let's do this, I suppose."

Sinking back onto the bed with her own poetry book, Ginny glanced at his furrowed brow and the slightly boyish expression he wore as he skimmed the pages. He looked up and she snapped her gaze away.

"This would be much easier at your father's house, you know," she ventured. "I have it on good authority you have an excellent library."

"Oh you have it on good authority do you?"

"You're not the only one who can ask questions about people. Everyone is quite keen to talk of the adventuring lord, you know."

"We're not going to my father's house," he said rather more coldly than she had anticipated. "And I bought what books I could find, hence me having to travel here by damned carriage."

The teasing crinkles around his eyes vanished and his lips remained in a firm line. She didn't know what it was about talking of his family, but it always transformed him, as though his bold personality and arrogance shrank away.

Perhaps his father had disowned him. That would explain why he needed the treasure so badly. He couldn't fund his bachelor lifestyle anymore. Though from the tired appearance of his clothing, he hardly seemed the sort to be racking up debts at the tailors, and she had yet to see him spend any money on anything but the essentials.

"You don't like carriages?"

"Too bloody enclosed and slow." He kept his head low over the book. "Anyway, your brother-in-law has a decent library."

"He's not my brother-in-law," she pointed out. "Not yet at least. And where do you think these books came from? But I refuse to get under his feet."

"Sweeting, if his estate is as big as any other country estate, I doubt you would be under his feet."

"The point is, I won't be an inconvenience to either my sister or Apollo." She flicked over a page. "They have been kind enough to offer me shelter without question."

And without dispatching her back home. There were few people she could think of who would accept her need to escape and even fewer who wouldn't be scandalized by her running away from an engagement. If anyone understood her need, though, it was Maisie. Although her sister escaped in less unseemly circumstances, Maisie had gone against the wishes of the family and created a life for herself full of love and fulfillment.

Ginny had only hoped for fulfillment. Love didn't really matter, she thought. Seeing Apollo and Maisie together, though, she wasn't so certain about that anymore.

"Having met your sister, I doubt she sees you as an inconvenience, Ginny," he said softly, and she glanced at Pierce.

His eyes were still fixed on the page, but there was a tenderness in his voice that made Ginny's heart skip a beat. She didn't know why his words affected her so, but she couldn't help the warmth that spread through her chest. She wasn't certain she'd ever felt loved. Maisie had been a lady's companion for much of Ginny's life, and no one else apart from her father understood her. The gap his death left had seemed unfillable.

But perhaps there was hope. Once she was certain Sir Horace had left England, she could work properly with her sister. Running an inn wasn't exactly her dream but she could get better at serving tables and taking orders. Maybe there would be time to continue her historic research on the side. Who knew? Perhaps even one day people would acknowledge that women were just as capable of producing quality research as men were.

She turned her attention back to the book as Pierce looked in her direction. She didn't know why, but for some reason, this bold, brash man made her feel anything was possible. It could well be worth putting up with his arrogance for just a little longer.

∞∞∞

Pierce snapped shut the book in his lap and stretched, then cracked his knuckles.

He caught Ginny's glare. "What?"

"You shouldn't do that."

"Do what?"

"Crack your knuckles." She nodded toward his hands. "Mr. Watts says it's bad for you."

"Mr. Watts? Is he a doctor?"

Her cheeks flushed with pink. "Well, no. He's a carpenter. But does it sound like a healthy noise?"

"All I know is that it makes my hands feel better, so how bad can it be?"

She nibbled on her bottom lip, and he tensed up expecting a new wave of dissent. But she merely returned to reading her book.

Sitting in a small room alone with her, silence around them, seemed so unnatural at first, yet after a while, Pierce found himself settling into the routine of it. It was almost as though he was seeing Ginny in her natural habitat. Whatever her previous life had been, he couldn't picture her sitting politely in drawing rooms or being swept around assembly rooms by potential suitors. This was where she belonged, her head buried in books, and an odd sense of reverence struck him when seeing her like this.

"What is it?" she asked, her finger pausing on a page, her head still lowered.

"Nothing."

"You're staring, Pierce."

Well he couldn't very well tell her he was trying to decide if she looked better climbing castle remains or delving through books, especially given she didn't really look wonderful doing anything in the awful, oversized boy's clothes.

"I was wondering why you still wear those clothes, even in private."

"I don't have any other clothes."

"Can't borrow a dress from your sister?"

She sighed and met his gaze. "She's rather differently shaped than me in case you had not noticed. Besides, there is no sense in risking changing clothes all the time." She wrinkled her nose. "Though trousers are not as freeing as I had expected them to be. I rather miss dresses at present."

Pierce never had cause to weigh up the benefits of men's clothing versus women's, but he never liked the idea of stays any more than he enjoyed wearing cravats. All of them were designed to be restrictive, and he couldn't fathom why anyone would want to wear them. He wasn't one for following fashion and it seemed a mighty waste of time.

"I suppose that makes sense," he said.

"I'm just grateful I have these clothes at all, truth be told. They're terrible, but they're better than nothing."

Pierce's mouth twisted in a wry smile. "I have to admit, they do suit you."

She raised an eyebrow. "Oh really? You think so?"

He shrugged. "They're not exactly flattering, but they do have a sort of...rugged charm to them."

Her lips twitched. "Rugged charm. Is that what you're calling it these days?"

He grinned at her, feeling a warmth creeping through his chest. He couldn't explain why he enjoyed teasing her so much, but something about the way she blushed and smiled made him feel strangely satisfied.

"You know, I could probably get you some more comfortable clothes," he continued. "My brother Peter was about your size when he was younger."

"I suspect I'll draw more attention wearing finery than what I have on now."

"And you don't want attention?"

She gestured up and down herself. "I've never had attention. Why should I want it to start now—whilst I'm hiding as a boy?"

Pierce didn't detect any wistfulness or sorrow that Ginny wasn't some elegant debutante drawing attention from the *ton* or the gossip columns, just a sort of acceptance that it was how things were. Given her sister was engaged to a viscount, he had to conclude their family wasn't entirely without connections, though running an inn was hardly considered a suitable job for a viscountess-to-be.

He could ask around again, he supposed, and dig deeper into her past in Oakfield but she wanted to remain hidden, and he didn't have it in him to reveal her. Not anymore at least.

"I don't imagine you know what it's like to be ignored."

She must have mistaken his silence for confusion, but she wasn't wrong. He couldn't recall a time when attention hadn't been on him. From birth, all eyes had been on him as the heir.

Now he didn't know if the stares were because he would one day be a duke or because of the tales of his adventures but he was used to it.

"At least take off that awful hat," he said instead of answering the question. "I've never seen such an ugly item of clothing."

Ginny put a hand to the cap and smiled slightly then drew it off. Her long golden hair spilled about her shoulders, cascading down like water finally breaking through a dam.

"Hair like that is hard to ignore," he said without thinking.

She fingered a lock. "I'm not really one for vanity but I've always enjoyed looking after it."

"A shame to keep it hidden away."

"It's only hair."

Hair that made his fingers twitch with the odd need to touch it. He stared at her until she looked away and he blinked rapidly. There were times he forgot she was a flesh and blood woman and in his mind, she was merely Ginny—a small, frustrating person full of information he wanted access to.

But in this tiny room, with the door closed, he couldn't think of her as anything other than a woman.

And he didn't like it one jot.

Chapter Eleven

Dusk settled over the bedroom, drawing in flickers of pink and orange through the window. Ginny glanced at Pierce and regretted it. What did she expect anyway? The man was already beautiful. When highlighted by the setting sun, the furrows in his brow and the lines of his jaw seemed more stark, more intriguing.

She swiftly looked away and rose, stretched her arms above her and lit the two candles on the fireplace before lighting the lamp next to her bed.

"It's time for a break," she declared, rubbing the aching knot of tension that had formed on the back of her neck.

There was only so long she could sit in this tiny room. Reading poetry. With Pierce.

It was the poetry that was most off-putting of course. Ginny thought of herself as fairly open to most forms of the written word, but poetry was rapidly becoming her least favorite.

"Agreed." Pierce gave a languid stretch from his seated position, reminding her just how much space the man took up in this room.

"I'll see what I can muster up downstairs." She hastened out before he could offer to follow her.

"Silly," she muttered to herself as she stomped downstairs. There was no reason to let the man affect her. He was arrogant enough as it was. He didn't need her swooning over him simply because he looked far too handsome when poring over a book.

She snapped a finger. It had to be the books. That was it. She adored books and research and when combined with a man who had no right looking the way he did, it caused confusion. If he was striding around, declaring the sketch was a map and teasing her about her ugly hat, she wouldn't even be thinking twice about him.

Ginny avoided the busy taproom and ducked straight into the kitchen where the scent of freshly baked pies lingered. She gave the cook a quick smile and moved quickly so as to not get in the way of what sounded to be a busy night, preparing a platter of cheese, bread, and honey, and she stopped briefly behind the bar to pour two ales.

With the plate balanced on one arm and the ales gripped uncomfortably in her hand, she made her way back up to the bedroom and paused at the door to take a deep breath.

The books. That's all it was. There was no need for her to get carried away marveling at how his strong hands cradled them carefully or how sometimes he seemed to get a far off look in his eyes as he scanned the text.

Because tomorrow, the spell would be gone. When they were no longer surrounded by the scent of leather and paper, she would be back to being annoyed by his conceit and barely able to put a finger on why sitting in a bedroom with him made her skin tingle from head to toe.

Before she could put a boot to the door, it swung open and Pierce grinned at her, ushering her in. "I heard your footsteps."

"You make it sound as though I'm some galumphing beast."

"They're distinctive," was all he said with a funny smile, and she was left wondering what on earth was distinctive about her footsteps. She'd have to listen hard next time she walked about the inn whilst it was quiet.

Pierce took the plate from her and set it on top of a pile of books. When she handed him an ale, he returned to his seat and took a long gulp from the tankard.

Ginny looked away as his throat bobbed and eased herself back onto the edge of the bed. He offered out the plate and she took a slice of bread, dipped it in the honey, and layered on a piece of cheese.

She took a bite, the sweetness mingling with the savoriness of the cheese, and closed her eyes. When she opened them, she found Pierce staring at her.

"What is it?"

"You made a sound." His words emerged slightly tense.

"A sound?"

"A...pleasurable sound."

She gulped, warmth flowing into her face. "Well, I like cheese and honey. It's..." She stared at the food in her hand. "It's comforting. When I was younger, I'd sneak down to the kitchen, and Cook always left me some cheese and honey out. I never really enjoyed the fine dining my mother preferred."

"I forget you did not remain here."

"I sometimes wish I did. Maisie had a more enjoyable childhood here than I did in London I feel."

"I see."

"Do you not have something you enjoy eating that brings you comfort?"

He scowled. "Porridge I suppose."

"Porridge?" She nearly spluttered on the words.

"Why is that so surprising?"

"I thought it might be some delicacy considering how well travelled you are."

"I have tried many a dish and some were delicious indeed but after trying so many flavors, sometimes one needs something simple, warm, and comforting."

"I bet you make pleasurable noises too when you eat porridge."

Pierce chuckled, the sound so warm in the tiny space it sent tingles down her spine. "I imagine I do actually."

After a few moments of eating and drinking in silence, she tapped the book nearest to her. "Do you think we should give up? Mary could have been speaking nonsense."

"If I never read another poem again I would be happy but it's all we have."

"I bet you could find some useful books at your family home," she said as innocently as she could muster, stroking an idle finger over the gold lettering of her copy of Metaphysical Lyrics and Poems.

Ginny wasn't going to confess she'd listened rather too intently to two ladies gossiping about Pierce and the vast estate he was set to inherit one day.

He straightened in his seat. She eyed the stiffening of his shoulders with a frown. He wouldn't be the first man wishing to escape his duties, however, she'd heard him talk of his family and he hardly seemed reluctant to see them.

"Perhaps you could take me with you soon," she suggested.

"No," he said sharply.

"It seems silly that we are scrabbling for resources when you have one of the country's best libraries at your fingertips."

"It's not the country's best."

"Well, my point is—"

"I'm not taking you to Marbury House and that's final," he snapped.

She blinked at the blunt statement. "Oh." Ginny mustered a strained smile. "I suppose you do not wish to impose on your family any more than I wish to impose on my sister and her fiancé." She swallowed, swiped the crumbs off her trousers, and flicked open the book. "I understand," she said softly.

Oh yes, she understood. He didn't want to be seen with her. Youssef was allowed to stay at Pierce's house but not her, it seemed. Perhaps it was her odd disguise or maybe he just didn't view her as a good enough friend. But regardless of the reason, Ginny was left feeling disappointed. She had hoped that maybe, just maybe, there was something more between them. But now it seemed like she was just another acquaintance to him, nothing special.

∞∞∞

If upsetting people bothered Pierce a great deal, he probably would not have achieved what he had in life. After all, going against his duty and discovering hidden treasures took a certain amount of courage and determination. But there was one thing that Pierce did not like, and that was seeing Ginny upset. He could see the disappointment in her eyes when he refused to take her to his father's house.

But he didn't need her involved in his life more than she already was. This unassuming woman kept popping into his thoughts too much as it was, and while he doubted Ginny would judge his father's mental state harshly, Pierce couldn't bear for her to see the duke at his worst. The very idea made an icy chill sweep through him.

He eyed the pucker of her brow as she flicked open a book. He needed to say something. Anything. Hell, he was known for being quite the charmer when needs be. Surely he could dispel the tension in the air with some well-placed words.

"Ginny, I—"

A thud resounded through the building, making the glass in the bedroom window rattled. Pierce rose.

"What the devil?"

Ginny flew across the room to the window and pressed her face against the glass. "A scuffle by the looks of it. Someone probably slammed the door."

"Should I do something?" He joined her in peering out of the window, aware of a slight wave of warmth and soapy scent washing over him as he moved close to her.

She bit down on her bottom lip. "Looks to be three men involved." She sighed. "Maisie will not be happy. The inn isn't known for fights."

He spied the two men facing down a third. None of them looked like the usual patrons at the inn and though Pierce could not claim to recognize every villager in Oakfield, they appeared to be strangers in their midst.

"I should go and see what's happening."

Ginny grabbed his arm before he moved away from the

window. "I don't think that's a good idea."

"Your sister isn't here is she?"

"Not tonight, no."

"Well, I'm hardly going to let the place go to wrack and ruin whilst she is gone."

Ginny's eyes widened. "It's not your job."

"She trusts me to take care of you—"

"Trusts might be putting it a little strongly—"

"I imagine she would prefer it if you were not in the vicinity of any fights." Pierce loosened the tight grip she had on his arm, removing each finger one-by-one.

"And *I* imagine she would prefer it if you weren't involved in any fights actually."

"I have no intention of getting involved."

"I'd prefer it too," she said softly.

He ignored the pang her words sent through him and most certainly shoved aside the silent triumphant thought that rattled through his mind.

She cared about him.

It didn't matter. He had people who cared about him. He didn't need this stubborn little chit added to that list. Life was complicated enough at the moment without him worrying about whether Ginny liked him or not.

"I'll be but a moment."

Pierce made his way downstairs and out into the cool night. Raised voices revealed the nature of the men's disagreement to be over money. Pierce rolled his eyes. He wished his sex weren't so predictable. It was always money or women.

As the three men squared up to one another again, Pierce slowly inserted himself in the space between them, palms raised.

"Perhaps we can take this elsewhere, gentlemen."

"Not a chance in hell," spat the tall chap standing by a redheaded companion who had inked markings on his knuckles. That didn't bode well. Most people with tattoos had spent time in prison or on the wrecks in London.

Pierce looked to the third man who flexed his fists.

"I don't want any trouble," Pierce said, raising his hands higher in a gesture of peace. "I just want to make sure everyone stays safe."

The tall man snorted, "And who are you supposed to be?"

"Just a concerned citizen," Pierce replied, keeping his tone calm and even.

The man sneered. "We don't need any help from you. Mind your own damn business."

Pierce took a step forward, his eyes locked on the man. "Step away or I'll make you," he said firmly.

The tall man glanced him over, his jaw ticking.

The other two men, however, were not interested in reasoning. The shorter companion lunged past Pierce, fists flying. Pierce stepped back, avoiding the blows. The tall man leapt into the fray and Pierce grimaced. Two against one wasn't fair, regardless of the reasoning behind the fight. He pushed up his sleeves and edged toward the fight.

Before he could lift a fist, Ginny appeared at his side, holding a bucket. Without hesitation, she threw the water on the fighting men, drenching them completely. All three froze and turned slowly to face her.

Her face was pale in the bright evening, her eyes wide. Pierce stepped immediately in front of her.

"You bloody little wretch." one of them snapped, swiping the water from his face.

"I'm not the one fighting in the streets," she retorted, and Pierce grimaced.

"Why you little—"

The tattooed man tried to grab Ginny, but Pierce reacted before he'd even thought about it with a sharp jab to the man's nose. Bone crunched and blood welled from the man's face as he stumbled back.

Pierce eyed the other two men and squared his shoulders. "Shall we leave this fight for another time?"

Several moments passed and Pierce kept his fists balled and

his muscles tight.

"He broke my nose," the tattooed man complained.

The tall man glanced at Pierce, then the other man and finally Ginny. "You've had worse," he muttered. "Let's go. We can do this another time."

The three men dispersed, and Pierce waited until he was certain they were gone before turning to Ginny.

"You should have stayed inside."

She dropped the bucket to the floor and thrust a finger at him. "You were going to get involved in that fight. I could see it."

"Only if I had to."

She moved closer and jabbed his chest with her finger. "It could have been three against one."

He shrugged and took her finger in his hand. "I've had worse odds."

When she glanced at her hand, he followed her gaze, noticing for the first time how their fingers had somehow become entwined.

"You shouldn't have put yourself in danger like that," he muttered gruffly, trying to quell the butterflies in his stomach.

"I couldn't just stand by and watch," she said softly, her eyes fixed on his.

Pierce felt something inside him crumble as he gazed into her eyes. He leaned in closer, his lips hovering just millimeters from hers. Even as his mind screamed at the insanity of it all, he knew that if he just moved a little closer, he could taste her.

And right now, he'd never wanted anything more.

Just as he moved to close the gap, Ginny gasped.

"The stars!" she declared, jumping away from him. "But of course!"

Pierce took a long, painful inhale and followed her gaze to the star-speckled sky. "The stars?"

"That's what those markings on the sketch are. They're stars!"

Her wide grin did nothing to dispel the regret eating into his gut. He'd wanted to kiss Ginny Beaufort more than he'd wanted anything else in the world, and all she could think about were the stars.

What a fine mess he'd found himself in.

Chapter Twelve

The night air wrapped around them, still and patient. In the distance, the occasional hoot of an owl punctuated their footsteps as Ginny and Pierce made their way up toward the stone circle, having abandoned the carriage some distance away on the road. Milky starlight coated the tops of the stones, like beacons guiding their steps.

Ginny paused to gather her breath and Pierce trudged on ahead. He'd barely issued a word since she'd begged him to bring her straight to the stones. Not even an argument. He'd merely shrugged and said they ought to hurry as it was getting late.

Tension burrowed itself through the excitement swirling in her belly. For a second or two, she thought Pierce had intended to kiss her after that fight. And she, fool that she was, had nearly leaned in and closed the gap. If it hadn't been for a quick glance up at the sky, she'd have done it too. She'd have pressed her mouth to those tempting firm lips and made herself look like a prize dolt.

She'd been wrong of course. A man like Pierce didn't kiss girls like her. Most men didn't kiss girls like her. She was too plain, too serious, too unassuming.

She'd never hungered to lure men in before but for once in her life, could she not be too beautiful or too captivating? Just for once?

Shaking her head, she made her way to where Pierce stood in the center of the circle. It was better she wasn't beautiful or captivating really. They were too different. Pierce actually wanting to kiss her would only make things more complicated. They carefully avoided any conversation about what might happen if they found the treasure but there was no ignoring the fact they had opposing opinions on the matter.

Hands to his hips, Pierce peered up at the sky. She looked away from him as her throat tightened. All around them were thousands upon thousands of twinkling stars huddled close together. The longer one looked, the more stars emerged until it appeared as if not an inch of black remained, so she kept her gaze to the sky. Thinking about how perfect his profile was or how wonderfully right he looked staring up at the stars would not help matters.

"Oh, a shooting star!" Ginny pointed, but it vanished in a moment.

Pierce smiled slightly and the tension in her muscles eased. She didn't know what to do with a serious, stern Pierce. An arrogant, smirking one was much easier to deal with.

"A night like this I wouldn't be surprised if we spot more."

"Where's the sketch?" she demanded.

"All business, aren't you, Miss Beaufort?"

"That's what I'm here for is it not?"

He gave a tilted smile and handed over the piece of paper. She unfolded it and scrunched up her nose as she eyed it under the starlight.

"We should have brought a candle."

"You were rather in a hurry, sweeting," Pierce reminded her.

"I have some paper..." She pressed a hand into her trouser pocket and pulled out the notes she'd made as they had been researching poems. "I don't suppose you have anything I can draw with, do you?"

"You're in luck." He shoved his hand inside his jacket and pulled out a pencil. "What's your plan?" he asked as he handed it over.

She took it from him, wishing she'd taken the time to wear gloves when their fingers brushed, and a tingling sensation shot down her arm.

Ginny dropped to the ground with a thump and craned to look up at the sky. "I'm going to draw the position of the main constellations." She waved the sketch at him. "The dots on the sketch...they're stars."

"So it's a map then?"

"No, it's..." She huffed out a breath. "It's a map of sorts perhaps."

"I knew it."

"But it's too dark to compare them so if I make a rudimentary sketch of the stars as they are tonight, perhaps we can figure out what it all means back at the inn."

"Perhaps we can do it quickly. It's getting darned cold."

Ginny nodded, already working on her sketch. It was difficult to see what she was drawing clearly in the dark, but she managed to trace the major constellations and mark the positions of the stars on the paper.

As Ginny finished up her sketch, a sudden gust of wind rattled the stones. She frowned and glanced up at the sky. Thick clouds were rolling in, blotting out the stars.

"We'd better get going," he said, holding out a hand to help Ginny to her feet.

"Right." She folded the paper and tucked it into her pocket before taking his hand and standing up.

He kept her hand in his as they made their way back down the hill toward the welcoming warmth of the lamps of Pierce's carriage. The heavens opened as they climbed in, pattering upon the roof, creating a deafening cacophony that prevented much conversation as to their next steps.

Ginny didn't mind. The excitement within her ebbed, soothed by the sound of the rain on the carriage and the rocking motion while it traversed the roads. Combined with the warm, comforting fragrance of Pierce and the late hour, Ginny could scarcely keep her eyes open. It was only when the carriage pulled to a halt, did she become aware of being pressed to Pierce's side, her cheek firmly upon his shoulder. Warmth crept up her neck and settled into her cheeks.

Straightening swiftly, she scrambled to open the door before he could reach past her to help. "I'll see you tomorrow?" she asked, barely looking back at him. "No need to come in! Too wet!" she said over the rain as she slammed the door shut behind her and dashed toward the inn.

She didn't even look back when she reached the shelter of the doorway to see if he watched her. She couldn't. He might see the foolish feelings written on her face and realize that she was beginning to like being near him far too much.

∞∞∞

Pierce ignored what had to be at least the third curious look Youssef sent his way that afternoon as they rode toward the castle.

The dull, damp day did nothing to make Pierce's heart any lighter. So much so that not even the sight of the ancient structure towering over the countryside brightened his mood. The wet gray stone seemed to fit his state of mind perfectly.

As they hitched their horses at the base of the castle mound, Pierce frowned at the sky. Another storm loomed on the horizon, casting a bruised hue over the heavens. At least, he supposed, that would keep Ginny safely inside.

Youssef followed his gaze to the ominous skies. "Remind me why we are returning here?"

"Because we might have missed something."

"And why did we not bring Ginny?"

"Because..." Pierce huffed out a breath.

Because if he was near her again, he might think about kissing her again, and that was not something he needed in his mind right now. He should be thinking of the treasure and nothing else. Not about her long lengths of hair or the furrow in her brow as she scoured books or the look of excitement glinting in her eyes as she made a discovery.

"Because?" Youssef prompted.

"Because there's no sense in her being out in this miserable weather."

Youssef pulled his coat tighter around his neck. "I suspect there is not much sense in us being out in it either. Is there a reason I must be punished alongside you?"

Pierce scowled. "Punished?"

"I've been your friend for a long time, Pierce. Bad news often equals a miserable hike or pushing on through a freezing night or following the trail that we were told we most definitely should not have done."

"If it's that hard work being my friend," Pierce grumbled, "perhaps you should return home."

"And give up the generous pay," Youssef scoffed. "Unlikely." His friend's face softened, and he put a hand on Pierce's shoulder before they could continue up the path toward the castle. "Nor should I wish to abandon you now, when your need is greatest."

"My need is not great." He looked at the castle. "I'm perfectly fine. And a walk up a hill in the rain is hardly some epic journey. I have no need of your help if you wish to return to the estate."

"Pierce..."

With a sigh, Pierce returned his attention to Youssef. "Yes?"

"Want to tell me what's going on? Is it your father?"

Pierce pressed his lips together. It *should* be about his father. It should be about his family. They needed to be his focus right now.

And yet...

"Or is it about something—or perhaps someone—else."

He shouldn't have even swung a surprised look his friend's way. They'd been on the edge of death and disaster enough time together to know each other better than brothers.

"I..." He swallowed, removed his hat and swept a hand through his damp hair, then placed it back on. "Well, I nearly kissed Ginny."

Instead of shock or surprise, a knowing spark appeared in Youssef's eyes.

"It wasn't just any kiss."

"It wasn't a kiss at all," Youssef pointed out.

"No." The ache of regret in his chest throbbed anew.

"But you wish it was."

"I shouldn't." He cursed under his breath. "Youssef, this felt different. This wasn't some fleeting attraction, or some need to sleep next to someone other than you."

"You're the one who snores."

Pierce ignored his friend's quip. "I felt it somewhere deep." He pressed a hand to his gut. "As though I was on the verge of discovering something new, something no one had ever found before."

"Perhaps you were." Youssef's lips curved. "But why didn't you make that discovery? It's not like you to make sensible decisions in the heat of the moment. From the way I've seen you looking at her, I'm surprised you did not ravage her then and there."

"The way I look at her? Whatever do you mean?" He shook his head. "She's dressed as a boy for God's sakes."

"She is not your typical beauty, I will give you that, but how many treasures have we found that would be passed over for nothing more than a dusty relic that turned out to be of great importance?"

Despite Pierce uttering his own doubts, he felt the need to leap to Ginny's defense. No, she would never make a debut at Almack's that would sweep Society off their feet, nor would she steal the attention of men everywhere she went. But that was only because the world was foolish, and they didn't see her intelligence or determination or—

"Damn it."

"She *is* worth more than a king's ransom then, eh?" Youssef said.

"No." Pierce jabbed a finger at his friend. "She's a fine girl but I've wanted to kiss women before. This feeling will pass."

"If you say so."

"It has to."

"Or does it?"

Pierce ignored Youssef's grin and set his head down against the increasing rain as he began to walk up the hill. Whether he wanted to kiss Ginny or not was irrelevant. He had his family to think of and she had, well, whatever had driven her into hiding to concern herself with. Besides, if he kissed her, she might think he had more than desire for her, and then she might try to persuade him to part with the treasure and do something hideously noble with it rather than use it to help his family out of their financial straits.

Teeth gritted, he kept his focus on putting one foot in front of the other, moving at a wicked pace that made his muscles ache and his lungs burn. Anything was better than picturing last night. Most especially when Ginny probably scarcely remembered the moment or—if she did, she remembered— running away from him into the inn.

If nothing else could persuade him of the folly of his thoughts, at least knowing she wanted nothing to do with being anywhere near him would help. He was in the business of wanting what no one thought could be found but he wasn't an idiot. Ginny didn't want kisses from him, and he was glad. It would put to rest any more of these thoughts and allow him to focus on why he was really here. His family needed him and that was all there was to it.

Chapter Thirteen

"Here, lad, isn't that my ale?"

Ginny blinked, dragged her attention from the inn door and hastened forward with the ale she clasped in one hand. She deposited it hastily in front of the man seated just in front of the bar and nearly spilled it all over the table. Wiping up the few droplets with her sleeve, she muttered an apology while the man grumbled.

The front door opened, and she stilled and watched the man in a greatcoat enter. As soon as he removed his hat, she let her shoulders drop.

Still no Pierce. And the day was growing late. It would be dark before long and their chance to go up to the stones to look at the stars would be gone.

What could have happened?

"Lad?" the man at the table waved a hand in front of her face. "You can get gone now. Don't need you lingering while I'm enjoying my drink."

Murmuring another apology, Ginny scarpered back to the bar. She'd been distracted all day thanks to Pierce. First it had been because the odd idea kept leaping into her mind that he looked like he'd been about to kiss her, and then it was because he'd failed to come to collect her to continue the hunt.

Maybe she'd insulted him by dashing off, but from what little she knew of Pierce, he wasn't the sort to be easily insulted.

Whatever it was, she wasn't impressed. He could have sent word at the very least if he did not need her.

Ginny's throat tightened and she rubbed the end of her nose. It had been too nice to be needed, blackmail or not.

"'Ere is that lad meant to be working or not?"

Ginny glanced at the bar to see the man she'd taken her time serving thrust a thumb in her direction.

"He's a bit bloody useless," he said to the barkeep.

The barkeep leaned in. "A charity case, I think," he said. "Miss Beaufort's given him lodgings, but the boy isn't here often. Always out and about." He shrugged. "What can I say, she's a charitable sort."

"He's making the place look a mess," the customer declared, looking straight at her. "All getting under your feet."

Grimacing, Ginny pushed away from the bar and made her way upstairs. The man wasn't necessarily wrong. She'd done a terrible job of helping at the inn today. Every time the door opened, or the sound of horse hooves echoed through the courtyard, her heart picked up speed. It had to be Pierce this time, surely? He had finally come get her so they could continue the hunt.

But no. Either he'd forgotten her or decided he no longer wanted her help.

She marched upstairs to her room to find the ginger cat her sister had adopted sitting on the windowsill. She joined her, spending a few moments watching a group of people exit a carriage while she fussed the animal.

"At least you want me," she told the cat.

The cat leaned into her hand, the comforting rumble of the cat's purr making Ginny smile for the first time that day.

As the carriage moved off, Ginny pressed her nose to the glass and peered at the sky. Another hour or so and it would be dark. At present there were only a few clouds and for all they knew, the stars could match the map tonight.

For all she knew, they already had last night. She had little idea because Pierce might as well have vanished. Short of turning up on the doorstep of his stately home, she wasn't certain what else she could do but wait.

The cat gave her a nudge when Ginny halted her petting of her, so she resumed her fussing of the animal.

"You're right, of course, June. I cannot simply just sit here and wait. What if he never comes back for me?" She smirked when the cat stared at her. "I know I sound pathetic, do I not? You wouldn't behave so uselessly I'm sure. If there was something you wanted, you would just go and get it."

Ginny sighed, her fingers curling around the cat's soft fur. June purred contently in response, as if offering her silent support.

Damn Pierce. Damn the man for ever discovering her. For making her think she was worth something more. For all she knew, she'd never see him again and these past few days of excitement would be a distant memory.

"No," she said softly, her breath misting upon the window. She rose so abruptly the cat jumped from the windowsill and forced its way out of the slightly ajar door. "No," she declared to her empty room.

She wasn't going to sit around any longer. She might have the key to finding the treasure and if she had to, she'd find it herself.

Ginny rose from the windowsill and straightened her trousers. She glanced at herself in the small mirror hanging on the wall, tucking a loose strand of hair back into her hat and snatching up the coat hanging from the back of a chair.

She dashed downstairs, doing up the coat as she went and fishing the gloves out of her pocket. It was a bit of a walk to the stone circle, but she had done it plenty of times in her youth. Now she just needed a lantern to ensure she could make her way back once it turned dark.

Smiling to herself, she retrieved one from the storeroom of the inn, and tucked the flint in her pocket. Tonight, she'd map the stars and she'd figure out what it all meant from memory if she had to, and she'd show the arrogant Earl of Beneford exactly who he was dealing with.

∞ ∞ ∞

"Is she with you?"

Pierce's gut sank like a stone. The only person Maisie could be speaking of was Ginny. Puddles collected in front of the woman's feet, her concerned expression highlighted by the warm light of the inn that cut through the increasingly dark evening. He dismounted swiftly and rushed toward the inn entrance, Youssef on his heels. He held a hand over his face to ward off the raindrops dripping from the brim of his hat.

"Ginny?"

"She's been gone since sundown." Maisie looked at Pierce then Youssef. "She's not with you?"

Pierce gritted his teeth. "No, but I think I know where she is."

The damned fool woman was determined to figure out what the map meant but he didn't think she'd be crazy enough to go out on this wet night. The clouds had cleared earlier but the rain hadn't stayed away for long.

"Stay here in case she returns," he told Youssef. "You can come find me at the stone circle if she does."

Youssef scowled. "She won't be there, surely? Not in this weather."

Aware of Maisie's proximity, Pierce didn't utter his worst fears. Heading out in the dark in this weather would leave her at risk of a multitude of dangers. Simply putting a foot wrong could wind up with her in a ditch and no roads were truly safe at night, not even on a night like tonight. What if someone had taken her? Harmed her?

"I'll bring her home," he said evenly, despite the pounding of his heart.

The rain worsened as he rode toward the stone circle, leaving the ground slick, forcing him to ride cautiously. What had been a grim afternoon, became black as coal.

Teeth gritted, he tried not to imagine her being snatched by some fiend for what little valuables she might have on her or lifeless on the side of the road. The gloomy night offered little by the way of guidance and if she had a lamp with her, he doubted it remained lit. For all he knew, she could have lost her way and not even be at the stone circle.

It was his best option, though. She had to be there. If she wasn't, he didn't know what he'd do.

The shadowy outline of the slope appeared ominous in the drizzle, and he squinted into the night to find the path worn by visitors in better weather, but had no luck in spotting it. Pierce opted to scrabble his way to the top, clawing at the mud, his breaths hot in the cold night.

Near the top, he started calling her name. The hoarse, desperate sound vanished under the pummeling rain.

"Ginny," he called again once he reached the top. He moved right into the center of the stones and bellowed her name.

What had she been thinking? What had *he* been thinking? He should have known she would not wait around at the inn for him in the vague hope he would come for her.

Pierce's heart raced as he scanned the darkened surroundings, hoping for any sign of Ginny. The rain continued to pour, drenching him to the bone, but he wouldn't give up.

He couldn't.

He circled around the stones, darting his gaze across the landscape, desperate for a glimpse of her familiar figure.

Just as Pierce's hope began to waver, a faint sound caught his attention. He paused and willed his heartbeat to still. He heard it again and turned toward the source.

He stared into the darkness until he saw a figure huddled against one of the towering stones. Relief flooded through him as he hurried toward Ginny's silhouette.

"Ginny!" he called out, his voice carrying over the howling wind. He approached cautiously in case she had injured herself in the treacherous conditions.

As Pierce drew closer, he could see that Ginny was shivering uncontrollably, her clothes clinging to her body. Her face was pale and sodden. He knelt beside her.

"Are you injured?" he asked, resisting the urge to haul her into his arms.

She shook her head. "No...j-just cold. I thought to stay here until the rain passed but then it didn't...and I-I..." Ginny met his gaze. "I feel weak, Pierce. I was scared that if I walked home, I would do myself more harm."

"You were right to stay here." He gave into temptation and undid the buttons of his coat to drag her into his hold. He wrapped his coat about her and flattened her cold, slender body against his.

"I knew you'd come," she whispered, pressing her head into the crook of his neck.

"Always."

Pierce held Ginny close, the desperate throb of his heart easing, despite the treacherous conditions. The rain continued to pound relentlessly, but in that moment, it seemed insignificant compared to the warmth radiating between them.

Gently, he brushed a strand of wet hair away from her face, his touch gentle against her cold skin. "You scared the hell out of me, sweeting," he murmured, his voice laced with concern.

She looked up at him and he suspected she was crying. "I'm sorry," she whispered, her voice barely audible over the howling wind. "I just... I needed to see if I could find answers."

"Let me get you out of here," Pierce said. "Can you walk?"

"Yes."

He helped Ginny to her feet and her legs wavered. He'd had enough. He needed her warm and his parents' house was nearer than the inn. Drawing off his coat, he slung it about her shoulders and did it up over her shaking body.

"W-won't you be cold?"

"No. My jacket is thick enough."

Sweeping her up into his arms and ignoring her gasp of surprise, Pierce picked his way slowly down the hill as though he was carrying some fragile treasure. How he didn't slip and harm them both, he didn't know. He allowed himself a sigh of relief when he reached his horse, though.

"I'm going to get you warm and safe, Ginny," he told her as he settled her across his lap and securely between his arms as he handled the reins. "And I'll be damned if you put yourself in harm's way ever again, do you hear me?"

She didn't respond but her warm breaths against his neck were enough to assure him she was well enough. For now. But that didn't mean he wouldn't ride like the devil was behind him to get her warm and comfortable because he'd never forgive himself if she ailed.

Chapter Fourteen

A warm weight prevented Ginny from rolling over in her bed. Had that cat snuck into her room again? She tried to pull the blanket from underneath the animal while keeping her eyes firmly scrunched shut, clinging to sleep she swore she still needed. Her bed was so warm, so welcoming and would be absolutely perfect were it not for that...

"Hey!" the cat said when Ginny gave it a nudge with her foot.

Snapping her eyes open, Ginny met the gaze of a wild-haired child who looked all too like Pierce.

"You're not a cat," Ginny said, her voice croakier than anticipated.

"I've been watching you." The child remained perched on the end of the bed.

"Uh..." Ginny shoved a strand of hair from her face, grimacing at how knotted and wiry it felt. "Thank you?"

The child smiled smugly. "I was making sure you didn't die."

"Well, I'm alive." She glanced around the beautifully appointed room in tones of muted greens and golds. Landscapes in heavy gilded frames hung on the walls and the canopy above the bed matched the tall gleaming curtains still pulled shut. A thin sliver of light slipped in between the curtain, hinting at it being daytime.

Her head gave a pulse pain and she put a hand to it. "At least I think I'm alive."

"My brother will be so relieved. He caused such a fuss last night when he brought you here, everyone in the house arose and *I'm* on the third floor near nanny."

"Oh."

Ginny felt her cheeks heat. She vaguely recalled the huge house, a few windows warm with lamplight beckoning her and Pierce toward it. Everything else after that was a bit of a blur. Had she really awoken Pierce's entire family?

The child jumped down from the bed and came directly to Ginny's side then put a tiny hand across her forehead. Ginny remained frozen, watching the furrow of concentration cross the pretty girl's face.

"I don't think you have a temperature. I suspect you'll live."

"I'm sorry I awoke you last night."

"Oh I'm not!" She grinned. "It was the most exciting thing to happen here since all the hens escaped and ran all over Mama's ornamental garden." She removed her hand from Ginny's forehead and rocked back onto her heels. "Why were you out in the weather last night?"

"I was..." Ginny sighed. It was all foolish and stupid and she heartily regretted it, especially now she had landed in Pierce's family home. "Well, I was trying to decipher a map."

"In the dark?"

"It's a map of the stars."

"Ohhh. You are helping Pierce, are you not?"

Ginny nodded. "At least I was meant to be." Him ignoring her for a day still stung and she doubted she had proved to him he needed her after last night.

"When did you meet my brother? Was it in Egypt?" The girl shook her head. "No, you don't look like you were in the sun. Are you from Norway?"

"I'm from England," Ginny clarified, unable to resist a slight smile. "I met him at the village inn."

"Why does he need your help?"

"I'm rather fond of history and I know the area better than him."

The girl pursed her lips and gave a succinct nod as though that answer satisfied her. "Pierce never spent much time here, but he said he's going to be around a lot more once he finds the treasure."

"What do you know of the treasure?"

"Oh only that an uncle I never met was searching for it forever and now Pierce is going to find it and then we won't have to worry about Papa not looking after us because Pierce will and —"

"Hettie." The stern tone in the doorway could only be that of Pierce's mother. Ginny's own mother had perfected saying her and Maisie's names in a similar manner.

"I think you need to leave Miss Beaufort in peace now," she continued. "She needs her rest."

"I was only making sure she wasn't dead," Hettie protested.

"And I think it's safe to say, she is not." She motioned to the door. "Come now."

"I'm glad you're not dead," Hettie whispered before Lady Marbury ushered her young daughter out of the room and firmly shut the door behind her.

Moving gracefully into the room, Lady Marbury smiled down upon her, revealing a few smile lines and crinkles around her eyes. Her hair was an ashen tone piled high, highlighting a long, elegant neck that led down to a figure most debutantes would be envious of. Ginny wondered if any member of Pierce's family was plain but concluded it was unlikely.

"I'm so sorry to be a burden." Ginny tugged the blankets high, only now realizing she was in a sheer chemise of some kind. Lord, she hoped Pierce didn't undress her.

"Not at all, Miss Beaufort. I'm only pleased to see you are well. My son tells me you have been aiding him in his search for this treasure."

"Well, yes—"

"And that it was during this search you became ill." She laced her hands together in front of her. "Pray tell me, Miss Beaufort, is my son wasting his time?"

"Wasting his time?"

"My husband's brother spent decades hunting for this

treasure. He became obsessed. Whilst I cannot declare I have enjoyed my son being far from home, it always relieved me that he never seemed to share that same fanaticism as his uncle." Lady Marbury paused, her gaze searching Ginny's face for answers. "But now he has you by his side, someone I am told, with knowledge and passion for history. Tell me, Miss Beaufort, does this treasure actually exist? And will Pierce find it?"

Ginny hesitated, unsure of how to respond. She didn't want to cause any worry or disappointment in Pierce's mother, but she also couldn't deny the truth. "Lady Marbury," she began cautiously, "I believe we have made discoveries that his uncle did not. As to whether this treasure is real, I cannot say. However, Lord Beneford is no fool and I trust his instincts completely."

The woman remained silent for a few moments, her lips pulled into a thin line. She released her hands from in front of her finally and her expression softened.

"Thank you for your honesty, Miss Beaufort. I appreciate your reassurance that Pierce's endeavors are not in vain." The duchess sighed and turned to look out the window. "My late brother-in-law, God rest his soul, was consumed by this treasure. It tore him apart, both mentally and physically. I fear for my son's wellbeing should he suffer the same fate."

"Your Grace," she began gently, "I am sure you know that Lord Beneford is a resilient and intelligent man. He has shown great determination and resourcefulness in our search thus far. I will do everything in my power to support him and ensure his safety."

Lady Marbury's eyes twinkled slightly as her smile broadened. "I believe you will do just that, Miss Beaufort." She put a hand to Ginny's arm. "But for now, you must regain your strength and I must let Pierce know you are awake. He only fell asleep in the parlor room an hour or so ago and that was after wearing a path in the carpet in the hallway."

Ginny swallowed hard and tried to keep any form of excitement from her face at the thought of seeing Pierce. He was worried for her because he didn't want to lose her help, nothing more.

∞∞∞

Pierce took the stairs two at a time, not even taking a moment to run a hand through his disheveled hair or straighten his shirt.

Hettie's excited declaration ran through his mind. *She's awake. She's alive.*

He couldn't imagine someone as stubborn as Ginny would die from a night in the cold but that hadn't stopped him from picturing her pale and lifeless and small in the grand bed of the east bedroom. He never wanted to go through a night like last night again.

"Ginny—" He froze after opening the bedroom door at the sight of pale shoulders. It took a moment for his brain to process the image in front of him, even as she gave a startled cry and clutched the chemise to her chest.

His mind finally caught up and realized he'd caught her in a state of undress. "Uh...sorry..." He swiftly backed out the door and clicked it shut.

Damn it.

Waiting outside the bedroom, he scowled to himself as images of sloped shoulders refused to leave his mind. Now how was he going to look her in the eye? He'd already behaved like an ass by leaving her at the inn and now he was making it worse.

Pierce raked a hand through his hair and took a deep breath. He needed to get himself together. Ginny was awake, that was what mattered.

The door finally clicked open, and he braced himself.

Somehow, nothing could prepare him for the sight of her in a luxurious silk gown. When she met his gaze, her cheeks pinkened and she glanced down at tiny matching lilac slippers that peeked out from under the lacy hem.

"Uh..." He swallowed. "Dress," was all he managed to say.

"I look ridiculous I'm sure."

"No…that is…it's a darned sight better than that awful floppy hat of yours." Inwardly, he winced when she shifted slightly.

All his worldly experience and he had lost his ability to compliment a woman.

"I'm assuming this belongs to one of your siblings."

He nodded.

"Will I get a chance to thank them?"

"Of course."

"And…" Ginny finally looked at him properly. "I must thank you, Pierce. I was reckless and impulsive, and I was frustrated but that was no excuse for worrying you…" She clapped hands to her cheeks. "Maisie! Oh goodness, she must be fretting."

Pierce took Ginny's wrists and removed her hands from her face then released her. "Maisie knows you are safe. I had word sent to the inn and Youssef was with her."

Ginny's shoulders dropped. "Oh thank goodness. I had better return swiftly, though—" She gnawed on her bottom lip. "Are my clothes dry?"

"They're probably still being laundered, why?"

"I cannot return to the inn like this. Someone might recognize me."

Sometimes Pierce forgot Ginny's situation was unusual. He forgot he'd figured out her disguise.

"You know I could help," he said softly.

She shook her head. "You cannot, and you have done enough already."

He chuckled. "Oh yes, blackmailing you into helping me and then ignoring you for a whole day is plenty."

"You still turned up when you were needed." She tilted her head. "I do not know what would have happened had you not arrived when you did, but, somehow, I just knew you would."

"Good. Now shall we go down to breakfast? Then we'll worry about finding your disguise."

"I'm being an imposition and your family—how on earth do I explain away my clothing last night?"

"Trust me, they are used to unusual occurrences. I'm not sure they even registered that you were dressed as a boy."

"I imagine Hettie did."

"Hettie notices everything," he agreed and offered out his arm. "And she likes you very much."

"I'm not sure what I've done to be liked but I like her very much too. She reminds me a little of me when I was a child. So full of questions."

Pierce grinned as Ginny took his arm. He rather wished he could have met little Ginny. No doubt she was smart and precocious and caused her parents endless grief with her questions and he'd have adored her.

He turned to lead her down the hallway and stilled. "Father."

The word echoed in the aching of his throat. His father looked more disheveled than Pierce and had been entirely unaware of the drama last night. His heart gave an unsteady jolt and he braced himself as his father beamed and made his way down the hallway toward them.

"Well, there you are, Diane!" He took Ginny's arms in his hands. "I've been looking all over for you. Did you see the goldfinches this morning? They've been quite enjoying the little treats you left them."

Pierce's heart dropped to his toes. It had been at least a decade since his sister Diane made treats for the birds and excitedly tracked them with Father.

"Father," he said softly when Ginny sent a confused look Pierce's way. "This is Ginny, not Diane."

His father ignored him. "We need to go look at the birds. You'll be thrilled to see how many there are."

"Father—"

Ginny sent Pierce a tiny shake of her head and smiled at his father. "I'd love to see them. Shall we?"

As his father excitedly chatted about the birds he'd seen, Pierce followed the pair downstairs and out into the gardens. His heart ached. He felt raw, exposed. Ginny had witnessed the one thing he needed to keep hidden. Even as Ginny indulged his father unquestioningly, the tension remained. He'd known Ginny's secret from the beginning, but he sure as hell didn't like her knowing his.

Chapter Fifteen

Ginny lifted her lantern and paused midway up the hill to look back at Pierce. "Stop looking at me like that."

He lifted his own lantern, highlighting his furrowed brow. "I'm behind you. How am I looking at you like anything?"

"I can *feel* it, Pierce."

"I have no idea what you mean."

"As soon as the clouds cleared you kept sending me these little looks as though I might fall into a swoon at any moment."

"Fine. Maybe I am a little concerned." He gestured about the countryside. "In case you have forgotten, last time I was here I was rescuing you from near death."

"I would never have died."

Ginny didn't know if that was true. Her mother was of the mind that a lady could die from the tiniest of chills. Ginny didn't really believe getting one's feet wet meant one could die. But as she had been curled up in the freezing rain, her limbs slowly turning from cold to lifeless, it had occurred to her that perhaps her mother was right.

It didn't matter, anyway. She was fine and Pierce had come for her, just as she concluded. Two days later, she wasn't certain why she had been so convinced he would come for her. After all, he'd abandoned her for the day and for all she knew, would never ask for her help again. Yet, the understanding he would save her burned brightly enough in her chest that she didn't even bother trying to make her way down the slippery hill in the pitch dark.

"You have to admit, Ginny, you were hardly full of life."

"A little warmth and rest and I am entirely well, and we've taken precautions today."

Though the weather remained clear, a few clouds lingered across the night sky, so they opted for extra warm clothes, lanterns in case the cool light of the moon vanished, and they'd all made a promise to return to the carriage on the road at the slightest hint of rain.

It was all a bit much really, however, Ginny agreed to it all just to remove the concerned look on Pierce's face. The last thing he needed was more to worry about it seemed. After meeting his father and his rather vivacious siblings, she understood that Pierce carried quite a weight up on his shoulders. They all relied on him, looked up to him, and he couldn't afford to falter.

Youssef came up behind them. "Thank you for waiting." He scowled at Pierce and took a long breath. "For once."

Pierce and Ginny shared a look. Neither would admit they had all but forgotten Youssef was with them.

"This better be worth it. I hope to never see a stone circle again," Youssef grumbled. "Or a hill for that matter."

Ginny glanced at the skies. "Look, Andromeda is there." She pointed toward the cluster of stars. "If my memory serves me, that lines up similarly with the map."

"Let's get to the top and find out for certain," Pierce suggested.

Once again they all gathered in the center of the circle, Pierce pulled out the map while Youssef held a lantern aloft. Ginny peered over Pierce's arm and pointed it to it.

"Look, Venus looks to be about as high as the map shows." She tapped a finger to the parchment. "And there's the north star."

Pierce frowned and twisted in a bid to align the map with the stars.

"Just turn a bit...no..." Ginny took the map from him, ignoring Youssef's chuckle and pivoted until the stars seemed to match the map.

"It does look almost the same." Youssef looked over her

shoulder. "But what does it mean."

Ginny stared at it for a few moments, her excitement ebbing. It perfectly matched the skies tonight yet what did it mean?

Pierce sighed. "Damn it. It's hopeless."

"No. Wait." Ginny grabbed Youssef's hand and lifted the lantern closer. "This isn't right."

Youssef groaned. "Please do not tell me I have to come back to this wretched hill another night."

"No, look there's an extra star." She pointed to the tiniest dot almost in the very center of the map, between lines that indicated the stones. "I've never seen such a star before."

"Maybe the map is wrong," Youssef said.

"Maybe it's like an *x*," Ginny proposed.

"An *x*?" Pierce leaned closer, the clean scent of him washing over her and tempting her to move even further into the warm strength of his chest.

She gave herself a little mental shake. She hadn't been able to forget how he'd cradled her or how wonderful it felt but that was to be expected, was it not? She'd been so cold and scared that night. Of course, his warmth and strong arms had been wonderful.

"Like how pirates mark their treasure," she said.

"I don't think pirates really do that," Pierce replied. "At least I've never seen a map like that."

"But maybe someone else did." She pointed between the two stones. "Maybe we're meant to go in that direction."

"So it's an x, marking the spot of the treasure," Pierce mused.

"It still doesn't mean much." Youssef sounded doubtful.

"It's more than we had before." Pierce took the map from her and moved toward the stones to look out in the direction to which the mark effectively pointed.

Ginny shadowed his footsteps and joined him at his side. "We go in that direction. Mark it carefully. See where it leads us." Excitement began to well up inside her. "This could be our next lead, Pierce."

He turned, set the lamp down on the ground and put both

hands to her cheeks. "I think you could be right," he said with a grin. "You bloody genius woman." He gave her a brief, firm kiss on the lips and released her before turning to stare out at the countryside.

She looked back to see if Youssef had noticed the kiss and thankfully the man had been staring up at the sky, muttering to himself. Ginny pressed a breath through her nose and willed her pulse to slow. It was only a celebratory kiss and Pierce hadn't even seemed to know what he was doing. No doubt, he'd forget it even happened.

And so she must forget it too.

She put a finger to her tingling lips and grimaced. That might be easier said than done.

∞∞∞

"Youssef, mark our position on the map." Pierce eyed the fence in front of them, hands to his hips.

"*Youssef, mark our position on the map,*" Youssef mimicked in a nasally tone.

Pierce ignored his friend. Youssef wasn't Youssef unless he grumbled about something at least once a day. In Egypt, their rollout beds were too soft. In Barbados, the sand was too coarse. England was most certainly too wet and too gray for the man. And today, he objected to being given the task of marking each step on the map.

Youssef's complaining was like the birds chittering every morning. Yes, one got awoken by them, but one would feel odd if there was an absence of them. And, of course, Youssef never failed to punctuate his complaints with a quick grin or a quip that left one never knowing if he was truly annoyed at the situation or just liked hearing the sound of his own voice.

"Perhaps we should go around," Ginny suggested.

Pierce shook his head. "I can't see a gate and we need to go as the crow flies or else we'll lose our path." He nodded to the fence.

"You go first. I'll lift you up."

"At least I'm wearing trousers, I suppose."

Pierce aided Ginny up and she climbed gingerly over the top of it and down the other side.

"Come on, you two," she said impatiently.

"Need a hand?" Pierce asked Youssef.

"Not on your life. I've been climbing things since before you were born."

Pierce waited as his friend huffed and grunted and made an inelegant show of dragging himself over the top of the fence and down. For a moment, Youssef wavered as he landed on both feet and Ginny jumped forward and steadied him.

Traversing the fence easily, Pierce jumped down and landed next to Youssef.

"Show off," his friend grumbled and trudged on in a straight line across the field, marking their position on the map.

Ginny tugged her trousers, adjusting the hems that had ridden up.

Pierce eyed her annoyed expression with a slanted smile. "The offer for me to find some of my brother's old clothes still stands, you know."

"And climb over fences in finery?" She laughed. "No, thank you."

"Perhaps you could give up your disguise," he suggested. "At least in our company."

Her face paled slightly. "No...that's not a good idea."

"If you told me what was going on, I might be able to help."

"No one can. I told you that already. Besides, I only need to stay like this for a little while longer, I think, and then I can get on with my life."

"And what exactly does that life look like?" Pierce shouldn't push for answers—after all, Ginny wasn't the only one keeping secrets.

Except, of course, Ginny now knew about his father, and he still had no idea why Ginny was living at her sister's inn, disguised as a boy. The funny thing was, if he really wanted to find out, he could probably write a few letters, see what anyone knew of Ginny Beaufort, but, in truth, he only wanted to hear her secret from her own lips.

For some reason, he wanted to earn her trust.

"I haven't quite figured that part out yet."

"Well, if it involves you staying in the county, I hope we can remain friends."

She blinked up at him. "Does that mean your adventuring days are over?"

"You saw how my father was," he said with a sigh. "I need to stay in England and look after my family."

"How long has he been like that?"

"A few years now." He shrugged slightly. "Long enough for it to be clear that my family cannot cope without me."

She put a hand to his arm. "I'm so sorry, Pierce. It cannot be easy to see him like that." Creases appeared between her brows. "Is that why you're so intent on finding this treasure? Will it help you look after your family?"

"Perhaps," was all he could bring himself to say. It was easy to talk to Ginny. Easier sometimes than talking to Youssef, but he wasn't the sort of man to spend his days complaining. He preferred solving his problems with action.

"Let's catch up to Youssef," Pierce suggested, changing the subject. "We don't want to lose sight of him."

Youssef had already walked most of the way across the field, pausing every now and then to mark his location.

"Youssef looks rather at home with a map," Ginny commented.

"Without him, I'd probably still be lost in Egypt."

"I think everyone needs a Youssef," she said with a smile.

"I agree."

"Did I hear you say you need me, Pierce?" Youssef turned to face them. "Perhaps my wages could reflect that fact?"

"You get paid a fortune," Pierce countered.

"In the meantime," Ginny said, "I am getting paid nothing at all."

"You have our company." Piece gestured between him and Youssef. "Is that not enough?"

She glanced them both over, a brow raised. "I rather think putting up with you both means you are now indebted to me."

"I'll put your name to the discovery when we find the treasure," Pierce vowed.

Her eyes widened. "In truth?"

He shrugged. "But of course."

Youssef rolled his eyes. "If we ever find it."

"We'll find it," Pierce said, unable to resist looking back at Ginny and wondering if her smile has always been that beautiful. "And when we do, everyone shall know Miss Ginny Beaufort helped."

She pressed her lips together, but she couldn't hide the excitement in her expression. "That will be payment enough, I suppose."

"Well, I don't want crediting," Youssef said. "Just pay me even more, and I'll be happy."

Pierce didn't care if his friend wanted his wages doubling at this point. All he could think about was Ginny's smile and how much he wanted to make her smile like that again. For a smile like that, he swore he was almost willing to give up the world.

Chapter Sixteen

The horse tugged gently against Ginny's grasp of the reins and shifted its weight. She understood the animal's impatience. For all they knew, they could have miles to cover in search of the treasure and none of them really knew what they were looking for.

She glanced around the empty inn courtyard and looked to Pierce. "What's taking Youssef so long?"

"He says English food doesn't agree with him."

"Oh." Ginny twirled a strand of hair that had escaped her hat. "I suppose I'm just anxious to get started. It feels like we could be searching the countryside for decades."

"I don't know if my uncle figured out what the star map was, but he certainly spent a lifetime searching for this horde."

"What makes you think we will have better luck?"

He grinned, his eyes glinting. "Because we have you."

He really needed to cease flattering her like that. It made her want to blush and simper under his attentions, and she'd never been one for blushing and simpering. It never seemed logical behavior to her. If one liked what someone was saying to them, one should simply say it.

Yet now she found herself unable to say what she really thought to Pierce. It all seemed a little ridiculous. She wanted to gush about how excited she was to be credited with finding the treasure or tell him how no one had ever said such flattering words to her. She longed to admit she had probably misjudged him in the beginning and explain how she saw he wasn't simply some adventurer looking to maintain his ego.

But what benefit would there be of her uttering such things aloud? He'd probably spent a lifetime hearing complimentary words. She'd just seem silly if she said such things.

Ginny sighed. "I hope that's true."

"Treasure seeking is a funny business," Pierce told her. "It's not nearly as exciting as it's made out to be and one can spend months scrabbling in the dirt or hunting out clues that turn into nothing, then suddenly it all comes together."

"I suppose it's like putting together a puzzle. You have all these scattered pieces, but once you find the right ones, it all starts to make sense."

"That's exactly it."

His tone held excitement that echoed the increasing anticipation she felt. To many, it must seem hopeless, but she supposed that was why ancient treasures remained hidden for so long. Only people like Pierce, with their determination and optimism could devote such time to hunting them out.

"Sometimes," he said, "the most unexpected piece is the one that unlocks the whole thing."

"I wish we had more information from your uncle. That would make life a lot easier."

"He was a cautious man, and rightly so. If the tales are true, this horde could be the most valuable discovering in the United Kingdom."

"Yes," she echoed, wishing she hadn't been reminded of the true reason why Pierce wished to find the treasure.

She understood his need now, yet she still didn't like the idea of it being sold to some rich lord somewhere who would hide it away forever, only bringing it out to boast to his guests how wonderful and rich he was.

Perhaps she could reason with him. He respected her opinion more now it seemed.

"I don't suppose—" Ginny turned at the sound of a carriage coming in through the arched doorway of the courtyard. She caught the briefest glimpse of a dark-haired man in the window of the landau. Her heart came to a shuddering stop.

He's found me.

Snatching Pierce's arm, she rushed toward the stables and darted inside, dragging him with her.

"Ginny, what the—"

Back flat against the brick of the building, she pulled him close and put a finger to his lips. "Be quiet," she hissed.

Pierce frowned but kept his mouth firmly shut while she listened to the footsteps in the courtyard. Sir Horace uttered something to his driver, but the words were muffled under the heavy thud of the pulse in her ears.

Pierce's hands found her arms and held her tight, his fingers a firm reassurance as she tried to concentrate on the warmth seeping through her jacket. Had he seen her? Would he recognize her? It had been years since the villagers had seen her, so it was easy to avoid detection. Horace had seen her only weeks ago and he was an astute man. She doubted a hat and some trousers would fool him.

Ginny met Pierce's concerned gaze as footsteps headed their way. They couldn't stay like this. Even in the dark of the stables, Horace would spot her, and there was nowhere to run.

"Kiss me," she said in a rush.

"What?"

"Kiss me!"

She curled her hands around Pierce's neck and dragged him down to her.

Pierce's eyes widened briefly. Then without hesitation, he closed the distance between them, his lips meeting hers in a desperate kiss.

The sound of footsteps drew nearer.

And the sound vanished. Lost to the heat and the firmness of his mouth moving across hers. Their mouths molded together, and for a fleeting moment, all thoughts of the intruder and their mission disappeared. It was just the two of them. Time seemed to stand still as his grip tightened on her arms and his chest pressed close to hers. She'd never felt so delicate and protected all at the same time.

"Good God," someone muttered, and the wonderful sensations shattered when she recognized the voice of Sir Horace.

Eyes firmly scrunched shut, Ginny tried to absorb the last few moments of the kiss as the footsteps retreated, but it was too late, the moment was gone, ruined by her fiancé.

Pierce slowly pulled away, his gaze searching hers. Ginny felt her face burning with embarrassment as she straightened her hat and adjusted her jacket.

"I'm sorry," she muttered, avoiding Pierce's gaze. "I didn't mean to... I just panicked."

"If we're unlucky, we'll be arrested for public indecency," he said with a wry grin that seemed to waver on his lips.

"It's highly improbable. The local magistrate is hardly motivated enough to leave their bed, let alone believe in a reported sighting of two men showing affection toward each other."

"Lucky for us."

"Yes. Lucky," she said, the words hollow.

She let her gaze linger on his mouth, aware of his grip still holding her firm. She couldn't believe she'd done that. Couldn't believe she'd tossed common sense to the wind and for the second time in her life, followed her instincts.

It could have very well been the biggest mistake of her life because she had a horrible suspicion she would never forget that kiss for the rest of her life.

And for a man like Pierce it was probably entirely forgettable.

∞∞∞∞

Strands of fair hair escaped that damned ugly cap Ginny wore, and Pierce had to fight the urge to rip it from her head, shove his hands into her hair and kiss her all over again.

The next time, he'd mean it. He wouldn't be taken by surprise, and he'd explore her mouth properly and savor the taste of her.

Except there wouldn't be a next time.

She'd only kissed him to hide from that man, he reminded himself.

He rubbed a hand across his face. "Do you care to explain why you didn't want that man to see you?"

"It was a mistake."

"The kiss?"

"No. Yes. I mean..." She blew out a breath, drawing his attention to lips that were still swollen. God, he wanted to taste them again.

"It wasn't who I thought it was," she said finally.

"And who exactly did you think it was?"

"It doesn't matter."

He tightened his jaw. His decision to leave it up to her whether she told him why she was in hiding began to feel entirely wrong. Was she being threatened somehow? Was she in danger? He wished she trusted him enough to let him protect her.

"I think it matters when you're dragging me into your business."

She blinked a few times, a flash of hurt crossing her expression. "Forgive me. It won't happen again."

Pierce grimaced inwardly. The terrible thing was, he wanted it to happen again. The opposite sex had never really been at the forefront of his mind. Courting and adventuring didn't go hand in hand. Yet as he looked at Ginny, he couldn't ignore the surge of desire that coursed through his veins. He'd led a reckless life to be sure but that had never really involved women. Caution had been his primary concern there.

However, there was something about Ginny that awakened a hunger in him, a hunger for connection and intimacy that he had never experienced before. It scared him, the way she made him feel so alive and vulnerable all at once. But he couldn't deny that he wanted more.

He just wished like hell he could understand where it all came from.

"I'm going to find Youssef," he muttered before he did something ridiculous like kiss her again. "Damned man is taking forever."

He pivoted on his heel as she declared she was staying in the stables. To remain hidden perhaps. He needed to escape but he wouldn't mind seeing if he could spot the man who had encountered them too. If Ginny wasn't going to tell him what was going on, maybe he could find out if she really was mistaken about the man.

When he ducked into the dimly lit inn, he spotted Youssef entering the tap room and waved at him.

"I need a drink," Pierce said, stopping at the bar.

Youssef glanced him over, brows raised. "I was gone for all of ten minutes. What on earth happened?"

"I kissed her, Youssef." He propped an elbow on the bar and rubbed his forehead. "I kissed her.

"Well, I'll be damned."

"Actually, she kissed me." He gestured to the barkeep. "Two whiskeys."

"Well, I'll be even more damned." Youssef looked around the room. "Where is she?"

"In the stables. Hiding I think."

"It was that bad, she's hiding from you?"

"From someone else."

He took the whiskey and offered his thanks to the barkeep then turned to lean against the wood to view the patrons. The man could be any number of people in the taproom, he realized. He'd been far too busy enjoying the feel of Ginny's mouth beneath his to see the man properly.

"Do we need to be worried?" Youssef asked.

"About the man?" Pierce shrugged. "Maybe. Whatever she's wrapped up in, it can't be good if she's hiding from someone."

"I meant more about the kiss."

"Oh yes, gravely worried."

"Because she won't help us anymore?"

Pierce shook his head. "No, because I liked it far too much."

A grin split Youssef's face and he gave Pierce's arm a nudge with his elbow. "That's no bad thing. She's a fine woman." Youssef ticked off his fingers. "She's clever, determined, able to tell you when you're being a fool..."

"And she's keeping secrets."

"Would you have told her about your father had she not come to your house?"

Pierce pressed his lips together. He couldn't say for certain. He'd spent so long being ashamed of his father's condition and so cautious about keeping it secret so no one took advantage, he couldn't fathom spilling all to anyone.

"Ginny's a good person," Youssef reminded him. "Whatever the reason is for her being in hiding, I'm sure it's a good one."

Pierce sighed and took a sip of his whiskey, his gaze fixed on the crowded taproom. Youssef had a point—Ginny had proven herself to be resourceful and trustworthy, even if she did keep things to herself.

But he needed answers. He needed to understand what she was hiding and why it had her so on edge. He had to protect Ginny from whatever danger she might be facing.

"If she doesn't tell me soon, I might have to find out what's going on for myself."

"She won't be happy about that," Youssef warned. "What if you put her in more danger by making enquiries?"

"Blast it all." Pierce tossed back the drink and set the glass on the bar top.

"Maybe if you kiss her properly, she'll give up her secrets."

"It *was* a proper kiss." Pierce ran a hand over his face. "And it can't happen again. She has secrets and I have a duty to my family. I can't let her get in the way of that."

Youssef lifted his hands. "As the English would say, it sounds like you're in a bit of a pickle, old chap."

"One could most certainly say that," Pierce agreed. "So we'd better find this treasure as quickly as possible so I can get myself out of it."

And far away from the baffling distraction that was Ginny.

Chapter Seventeen

Ginny ignored the desire to pout and fold her arms and sulk in the corner of the bedroom as her sister shook her head in a way only a disapproving older sister could.

"Surely you did not think you could hide here forever, Ginny?"

Ginny leaned closer to the mirror as she tied the laces of her shirt. She pulled the knot tight then turned to face the disapproving expression head on. When not just a mere reflection, the look did work. Ginny really, really wanted to slink away like a naughty little sister.

She forced herself to lift her chin. "He's probably just being a stubborn man. Wants to give me a telling off perhaps."

"It's not just Sir Horace." Maisie issued a frustrated breath. "I received a letter from Mama now. She knows you're not with our cousins. It seems Sir Horace already visited with them."

"Blast." Ginny retrieved her jacket from the back of the chair and shoved one arm then the next into it. "He only wanted to find his carriage."

"Which he found. Abandoned in some alley with half the wheels missing apparently. He's mightily furious, Ginny." Maisie pinched the bridge of her nose. "I can't believe you stole his carriage."

"*Borrowed.*"

"Running away from your betrothed, stealing a carriage, and now this treasure business. Not to mention the fact you are spending so much time with someone so...so..."

Handsome? Fun? Determined? Courageous? Ginny could think of any number of wonderful words to describe Pierce.

And their kiss.

She wasn't going to mention that to Maisie, though. She was already in enough trouble as it was.

"Scandalous." Her sister's expression grew troubled. "This isn't like you, Ginny."

It wasn't. Ginny never did things like run away from duty or demand kisses from ridiculously handsome men.

But she had to admit, she rather liked this Ginny. For the first time in her life, she didn't picture a life of a staid spinster or a meek wife that might, just might get to aid her husband in his career with the remotest possibility that it meant her life meant something.

"I didn't like lying to Sir Horace," her sister said.

"But I am grateful you did."

"He still wants to marry you, you know."

"I rather doubt it," Ginny said with less confidence than she felt.

Truth be told, were it not for hunting down this treasure, she might have returned home by now to face whatever she must, assuming that Sir Horace decided she was not worth the trouble.

It seemed Sir Horace had *not* decided such a thing.

Maisie sank onto the bed. "I was surprised when I heard of your engagement to him but knowing of his expertise in history, I understood the logic behind accepting his proposal."

Ginny did up the buttons of her jacket, avoiding her sister's gaze.

"Now, considering I have lied to not only Sir Horace but our mother and brother, will you tell me exactly why you saw fit to run away from him?"

A knot gathered in her throat when she recalled her first encounter alone with Sir Horace at her brother's house in London. She hadn't expected the man to be overawed with her, but his smirking words had been entirely unanticipated.

As had the way he grabbed her arm, his fingers sinking deep into her skin and leaving bruises that lingered during her first few days in Oakfield.

She had to wonder if the man would leave more bruises in future.

Ginny tried to swallow past the knot and her voice came out tinny as she told her sister, "He laughed at me."

"Laughed at you?"

"I told him how excited I was to aid him in his research and how I hoped I could be useful to him in his work."

"And he laughed at you?"

"Yes."

Maisie opened her mouth then closed it. "Well, that's not terrible but—"

"He told me I was to be nothing more than a broodmare. That I would be hidden away in Scotland somewhere, never to be seen." Ginny's entire body heated with humiliation as she heard the words all over again in her mind. "I'm too plain to be seen with him, it seems."

Maisie's eyes widened. "He called you plain?"

"That's a polite way of putting it." Ginny stared at the tired brown boots on her feet. "Let's just say, he made it clear he was only marrying me because of my connection to a soon-to-be viscountess and our brother, and that he had no intention of letting me back out of the arrangement."

"A gentleman should always allow a lady to change her mind."

"He's no gentleman."

"No," Maisie agreed. "And now I'm rather regretting being polite to him."

Ginny met her sister's gaze and forced a wobbly smile. "It doesn't matter anyway. I'm certain he'll realize it's much easier to find a wife who hasn't run away and give up on me soon."

∞∞∞

Heart pounding in his chest, Pierce stared at the dark ceiling, just able to make out the cornicing at the edges of the room. He couldn't have fallen asleep that long ago. His mouth was dry and his eyes gritty from a night of tossing and turning and being unable to cease replaying that kiss in his mind.

The kiss could also be responsible for his pulse beating like a war drum, but he had a vague recollection of hearing something.

He waited there, in the dark, guessing it to be the early hours of the morning. Once the thud in his ears dimmed, the only sound he could make out was the slight gush of wind and the occasional hoot of an owl in the distance.

Rolling onto his side, Pierce fought with his pillow for a while before giving up and throwing back the covers. Who was he kidding? Sleep wasn't going to come anytime soon. He blindly groped for his dressing gown, shoved his arms into it and did it up tightly before heading out into the hallway. He made his way to the top of the stairs and paused when he saw flickering light coming from his parents' wing.

He heard it then—a strange, plaintive cry that returned his heart back to pounding.

Pierce headed straight to the source of the light. The door to his father's room remained ajar and the sound came again, echoing about the hallway. He inched open the door to find his mother on his father's bed with his father held tightly in her embrace.

His father's face revealed a mask of pain and anguish as he let out another yowl like a wounded animal.

His mother gasped when she spotted Pierce. "Go to bed," she said in a harsh whisper.

"What's going on?" Pierce demanded.

"It's nothing."

His father trembled from head to toe, his gaze darting about the room but never fixing upon anything.

Pierce stepped fully into the room and closed the door gently. He didn't want his siblings seeing this—especially little Hester.

"This happens a lot, Pierce," his mother said with a sigh. "I can manage it."

He swallowed hard and looked between the man who had once seemed so strong, so in command of the family, and his mother who he always recalled moving about the house as though she was skating on ice, all silk and feathers and glamor.

All he could see was strain and exhaustion and pain.

"Please," his mother insisted. "It won't help that you're here. Just go back to bed."

He hesitated then nodded. While he'd been away, his mother had been handling his father's mental decline with grace and Pierce couldn't deny she knew better how to manage it than him. He slipped out of the room and propped himself up against the wall while he resisted the desire to pace.

He'd known things were bad. Terrible even. But he'd never seen either of his parents look so aged, so fragile.

He didn't like it.

After what had to be about half an hour, his mother emerged out of the room with a candle in hand. She closed the door gently and offered Pierce a tight smile.

"He should be fine for the rest of the night. Go back to bed, my darling."

"How often does this happen?"

She glanced at the floor then met his gaze. "A few nights a week."

"You must be exhausted, Mother."

"It's nothing I cannot manage. I raised a great many children if you recall."

"With the help of a nursemaid."

"Do you think a nursemaid could soothe away your nightmares?" she scoffed. "None of you would be satisfied with the embrace of bony Mrs. Mason if you recall?"

Pierce vaguely recollected his mother coming in to give him a hug in the middle of the night when he was a boy.

"She was like hugging a skeleton." He gave a shudder. "But Hester is grown now, and it's been a while since you've had sleepless nights."

"If you tell me I'm too old for this, I'm not past putting you over my knee." His mother wagged a finger at him.

"You shouldn't be having to do this."

She set the candle on the nearby vase stand and took Pierce's arms in her hands. "If I do not, who will? A nurse cannot soothe him the way I do." Her expression softened. "Besides, I made vows to your father. And I shall see those vows through 'till the very end."

Pierce appreciated the affectionate example of marriage his parents made. Too many of his friends at Eton had parents who could scarcely stand to be in the room together.

"Dr. Thorne thinks we should go to the coast," his mother admitted. "See if the sea air helps."

"It's too risky."

"I agree. We are in a financially precarious situation as it is. Should anyone think your father is not the strength of this family, investments could be withdrawn, and debts demanded back."

The night began to close in on Pierce, as though weighing on his shoulders like a ten-ton blanket. Here he was, lying around thinking of kissing Ginny and his mother was spending sleepless nights soothing her husband while their world fell apart around them.

"You won't have to worry about our finances soon, Mother," he vowed.

Pierce's mother smiled sadly, her eyes filled with gratitude. "Oh, my darling, we will weather the storm no matter what, but I am grateful to have you home." She reached out and squeezed his hand. "Your siblings have always admired you, Pierce. And I am so proud of the man you have become."

He nodded, his throat constricting with a mixture of emotions. Guilt for not being there when his parents needed him most. Anger at the world that had dealt them this cruel hand. Determination to do whatever it took to protect his family and preserve their legacy.

He glanced at the vague shadow of the portrait of a great-great relative of some sort. "I refuse to let our name be tarnished or our history slip through our fingers."

She looked at him with tear-filled eyes and squeezed his hand again. "I know." She released his hand, retrieved the candle, and moved onto tiptoes to kiss his cheek. "Now go get some rest. You have treasure to find still, remember?"

He nodded and watched her head back to her room before returning to his own. If life wanted to light a fire under his rear, it had done a fine job. He couldn't let his mother suffer the strain of not only dealing with her husband but also worrying for the fate of their family any longer. He needed to find this treasure now.

Chapter Eighteen

The bright rays of the sun illuminated the vibrant green fields stretched out in front of Ginny, casting a warm glow over everything. Fluffy clouds drifted lazily, providing a welcome contrast to the clear blue expanse. Though the day was bitter, she turned her face briefly to the sky, welcoming the break from the rain that had plagued them all last week.

The three of them moved at a slow pace on horseback with Youssef continuing to mark their position. To look at the countryside, marked with clusters of trees and lined with hedgerows and the lines of the farmer's ploughs, one could never imagine there might be treasure somewhere amongst it. A wide river wound in a glittering ribbon guided their path onward, the water rushing past far faster than they could move.

Ginny might admit that she felt rather hopeless about it all if it were not for Pierce's renewed determination.

This was what treasure hunts were about, he insisted. Days and weeks of nothing, of one's hope waning before being sparked again by a discovery.

She tried not to keep stealing glances his way, but he made it so difficult, sitting so proud and determined upon his horse. His greatcoat highlighted strong shoulders that made her fingers curl around the reins as the desire to feel the strength of him sat low in her belly.

It was all thanks to that wretched kiss. If she had remained in ignorance as to what his mouth and body could feel like, she wouldn't be so distracted. Logically, he was the same golden-haired, devilishly handsome man she'd first met—and disliked.

But everything had changed now. Sensations she'd never experienced and never expected to experience kept running through her, sending shivers through her body.

Ginny sighed aloud. What had she been thinking yesterday? This was an utter disaster. In her panic, she'd made a huge mistake and at this point, she was starting to wonder if it was not easier to give herself up to Horace. Perhaps when he saw the lengths to which she had gone to hide, he would realize she wasn't worth the effort.

Though from what her sister said, Ginny had offended his pride greatly. Her experience of the opposite sex was not vast, however, she'd met with enough of her brother's friends to know that men of great ego did not take well to being rejected.

"Never fear, Ginny," Youssef said, and she realized he must have heard her sigh. "Not every day will be like this."

She gave a thin smile.

"At least it's not raining," he said brightly.

"Very true," she agreed, and they slowed as Pierce came to a halt at the edge of the river.

A small bridge which was no more than planks of wood bound together with frayed, mossy rope finally gave them a chance to cross the river.

Pierce dismounted and Ginny followed suit to join him as he eyed the bridge with hands to his hips.

Ginny nibbled on the end of her thumb. "It looks old."

"And weak," Youssef added.

"Perhaps we should find another way over," she suggested.

Pierce shook his head. "I can't see another crossing nearby. Is there anything on the map?"

Youssef puffed out a breath. "The only proper bridge marked is several miles away. It takes us west by quite a bit."

"According to my grandmother, the river used to flow closer to the next town, but a storm broke the banks, and it carved a new path." Ginny eyed the slippery looking planks. "Not that

that helps us now," she said with a laugh, feeling ridiculous for even mentioning it.

"That would have made life much easier for us." Pierce marched off, leaving Ginny and Youssef to watch him retrieve a large branch from the nearby row of trees. He leaned over the river edge and dropped the end of the branch into the gushing water.

His brow furrowed. "Too deep for the horses."

"Too fast too," Youssef said.

"I'll go across," Pierce announced. "Maybe it's stronger than it looks."

"Be careful." She held her breath as he put his boot to the first plank and nearly slipped.

"Just a little slippery," he said as he regained his balance. "Don't worry. I have no intention of taking a dip." He gave her a wink that made her heart flutter in her chest.

Youssef leaned in. "I'm not rescuing him if he falls in."

Ginny had long suspected Youssef would do anything for his friend. The fact he followed him around the world spoke volumes.

"I've spent too many days getting wet," she agreed with a grin.

"I heard that," Pierce said. "What wonderful friends I have." He stepped lightly over the next few planks and paused. "I think it's fine but I'm not certain it will hold the horses weight."

"There's a farmhouse back there." Youssef thrust a thumb backwards. "I reckon I can persuade someone to look after the horses for the day while we continue on foot."

Pierce held out a gloved hand and motioned for Ginny to follow him. "You first, sweeting. I have no desire to be going in after you either."

She stepped onto the first plank and her foot slipped instantly. She snatched Pierce's outstretched hand and righted herself with a hand to her thudding chest.

He led them forward a few more steps and an ominous crack sounded. Ginny glanced down at the rushing water and wondered if she could really outswim such a deep, fast river.

"Quickly," Pierce said and dragged her forward.

The bridge gave way underneath her as she ran. In a blur of movement Pierce yanked her by her wrists and tossed her as though she were nothing more than an empty grain sack onto the grass. She rolled over to spot him diving forward as the bridge vanished. Her heart stopped for a brief moment, and she waited for the splash.

Pierce's head appeared over the embankment and Youssef laughed. "You're a damned lucky fool."

Pierce crawled his way over to her. "Are you well?"

"Fine. You?"

"Not wet which is good." He grunted as he rose to his feet. "Make your way to that bridge," he told Youssef. "We'll meet you there."

"I'll have to follow the road. You'll probably beat me there."

Pierce nodded and brushed the grass from his coat then offered Ginny a hand to help her up.

"Looks like it's just you and me."

The apprehension in his gaze echoed the strange, tangling sensation in her throat. She wasn't certain why a renowned rake who had women practically drooling over him everywhere he went should be bothered by that statement, but maybe he feared she would do something reckless like kiss him again.

Well, she was no glutton for punishment and while his kisses certainly couldn't feel farther from punishment, the tension afterwards did. Ginny silently vowed that no matter what, he would not suffer from any further attempted kisses from her.

∞∞∞

Apart from wet boots and grass stains smeared across Pierce's breeches, he had technically come away from the bridge collapse relatively unscathed. However, he reckoned a piece of wood might have scratched him as his side stung. He could hardly complain, though, given no one had ended up taking a dunk.

He glanced back at the churning river. He'd taken greater risks in the past but this time he had Ginny with him.

And he had a family relying on him.

Of course, now he also had to contend with being alone with Ginny yet again. He'd laugh if he wasn't so apprehensive about being alone with her. Someone up there was toying with him.

He glanced at her matching grass stains and smirked as she straightened her ugly hat. Who could have known temptation would come in such a strange, plain bundle?

Who would have thought he would barely have enough restraint to resist her?

He could blame the rush that still coursed through his blood or perhaps how close she had come to plunging into the river. He could blame the stresses of managing his family. Maybe he could even blame the fact he couldn't remember the last time he'd kissed a woman anymore.

It would all be lies.

It was her. It was her lips. The feel of her crushed against him. The way her hands wound about his neck and the little sounds she made as he explored her mouth.

It was all her.

"Should we get moving?" she said, and he blinked.

"Uh. Yes. Let's."

He took a last look at Youssef leading the horses toward the road with regret. At least with him with them, Pierce could ignore the pull in his gut that said he'd never find another woman like Ginny.

It could well be true. He seldom ignored his gut. But if there was ever an inappropriate time to meet the woman of his dreams, it was now. Not only did she have her secrets, but she would also want him to give up the treasure, and he had a horrible feeling he'd want to do that for her.

No. He shook his head to himself. He had to be stronger than this. His family deserved better.

They trudged in silence for a while, the sound of their boots swishing through the grass seemed to amplify the weight of the unspoken words hanging in the air.

Ginny stopped and put her hands to her hips. "I still don't see the bridge."

Pierce hissed out a breath. "I should have taken the map from Youssef before crossing." He made a face as he twisted and the scratch on his side rubbed against the material of his clothing.

"Pierce?"

"It's nothing."

"Are you hurt?"

"Just a scratch." He rubbed his side. "Must have caught myself on the bridge or something."

"Let me see."

Her hands were upon him before he could bat them away. Ginny tugged at his clothing, shoving apart his jacket and pulling his shirt from his waistband, leaving his skin bare to the air. He looked at her closely then, watching lashes dart across her cheeks and spied a few new freckles dashing across her nose from her time in today's sun.

He wanted to kiss them.

He wanted to kiss her.

He inhaled deeply and bunched his hands into fists, allowing her perusal of him.

"Oh, it really is just a scratch."

He lifted his shirt and eyed the red mark. "Won't even scar."

Her fingers danced across his skin, closer to his hip and every muscle in his body tensed.

"This did, though. How on earth did you do that?"

Both of her hands lingered on his waist, oh so casually and oh so comfortably, as though they knew each other's bodies intimately.

I wish.

"Youssef fell on me." He frowned. "I think."

Ginny bent to eye the scar more closely, her eyes wide. "How did Youssef falling on you cause this?"

"We were climbing down into a tomb and his grip gave way. Took me down with him and I landed on something sharp."

She sucked in a breath. "Ouch."

"It's not the worst." He tried to swallow past his dry throat and tried to figure out quite how he had found himself in this situation.

"What was your worst injury then?"

Yes. This was better. She'd given him a reason to remove her hands from him even if he wanted her touch more than his next breath. Pierce took her wrists and eased her hands from him, ignoring how cold he felt without her touch. He rearranged his shirt and pulled up the sleeve of his coat and jacket to reveal puckered skin on his forearm.

"Oh my goodness." She skimmed a finger over the sizeable scar. "This looks like a burn."

He nodded.

"Did you get caught in a wildfire? Or perhaps your sleeve caught on a torch?"

He smirked and shook his head. "I caused a pan fire."

Her gaze lifted to his, her brow puckered. "A pan fire?"

"Safe to say, Youssef doesn't let me cook anymore."

Her lips curved. "That isn't a very heroic story."

It was no good. Somehow, he'd been able to resist her touching him but when it came to a smile that crinkled the corners of her eyes, he couldn't resist.

Maybe she couldn't either. He swore she lifted her chin almost imperceptibly. Really, it didn't matter who made the first move, because the end result was the same.

Pierce curved a hand around her neck and pressed his mouth firmly to hers.

Chapter Nineteen

Ginny's mind blanked as his lips molded against hers with a hunger she couldn't deny. The scratch on his side forgotten, the scars on his arm irrelevant. All that mattered was the way his mouth moved against hers, the way his hands gripped her tightly, pulling her closer.

Her resolve shattered like glass, and she found herself responding to him with equal fervor. The tangling sensation in her throat dissolved, replaced by a desire that consumed all rational thought. In that moment, she couldn't fathom why she had ever vowed not to kiss him again.

His fingers tangled in her hair and his tongue sought hers as he deepened the kiss. A soft moan escaped Ginny's lips, lost in the sensation of Pierce's mouth on hers.

But just as quickly as it had begun, Pierce abruptly pulled away, leaving her feeling cold and bereft. His hands dropped from her, as if he had been burned by their touch.

"Ginny, I—" He ran a hand over his face. "I can't keep kissing you."

She shoved her hands into her jacket pockets to hide how they trembled. "I rather think I kissed you the first time," she said quietly and looked at the grass underfoot.

"Regardless, it was a mistake. There's too much…" He sighed. "I cannot afford to be distracted and you—"

"I have my own worries," she agreed, avoiding his gaze.

She didn't like keeping secrets from him anymore, but she had begun to understand that Pierce was not just some rakish adventurer. He had a big heart and would do anything for those he cared for. She suspected she might be one of those people now and she could not have him doing something ridiculous like calling Horace out for a duel.

"We'll simply make certain it does not happen again," he declared.

"Indeed."

"It's hardly a difficult thing, making certain one's lips do not meet, after all." He chuckled but his tone was strained.

"Yes. Absolutely."

Pierce cleared his throat and gestured along the faint line carved by feet through the grass that would eventually lead them to the bridge. "We should probably make haste. We don't want to leave Youssef waiting."

Ginny simply nodded. She wasn't certain she trusted herself with words. The idea of never experiencing his kiss again made her feel sick to her stomach. Where all this desire was coming from, she did not know, but she understood one thing...Pierce was responsible. This awakening was entirely down to him.

A small part of her feared she'd never feel such things again. It had been easy to resign herself to a life of making herself useful as a wife even if there was no desire or real love there when she hadn't ever been kissed in such a manner.

Now, even if Horace came to her and proposed the sort of match she had hoped for, she wasn't certain she could take it.

They resumed their trek but the tension between them remained palpable in the air. She stole glances at Pierce, noticing the way his brow furrowed and his jaw clenched. She supposed it was comforting that he seemed to struggle with this desire as much as she did. Someone like her never expected the attentions of someone like Pierce, yet she didn't doubt the sincerity behind his actions. The more she knew about him, the more she understood—he did nothing unless he was passionate about it.

Which meant he held some passion for her.

The thought made her entire body warm, and she forced her gaze to the horizon, scanning the gently rolling hills for a sign of the bridge or Youssef enjoying a leisurely ride along the road.

Narrowing her gaze at an odd shape in the ground ahead, she slowed her pace. She didn't know this part of the county that well. When she'd grown up here, she was only allowed a few miles from home.

Pierce paused and twisted. "Are you coming?"

"No." She marched past him and headed away from the river toward the rise in the field that soon revealed itself to be a stone covered in moss and overgrowth.

Pierce came up behind her. "What—" He sucked in a sharp breath. "Another standing stone?"

With trembling hands, Ginny scraped away the moss and weeds. There was nothing on the stone but there was no denying it was not a natural part of the landscape.

She looked at him, unable to keep the excitement curving her lips. "A marker?"

He grinned. "Maybe."

"Are we on the right path still?"

"It's hard to say without the map." Ginny eyed the path they had walked and wished they could still see the original stone circle.

"We'll have to come back once we meet with Youssef."

"No." She grabbed Pierce's arm. "Look, there's more." She scuffed aside the dirt with her boot to find one stone and then another. She spotted several more strange lumps in the field and followed the path that led them toward the edge of the woods.

"A good hiding place," she murmured.

"Let's go in."

Pierce led the way into the forest. The air felt cooler in the forest, the scent of pine mingling with the earthy fragrance of damp leaves. The sunlight peeked through the dense canopy, casting ethereal rays of light that danced among the trees but there were no more stone markers to be seen.

Pierce stopped and shook his head. "Perhaps they were leading from the forest to—" His brows furrowed. "No. Look."

She followed his gaze to spy a large mound of stone, similar in color to the markers they'd been following. They rushed over and Ginny ran her hand over the ivy crawling over the formation that rose up out of the ground. Frowning when the ivy gave way under her hand, she tore some aside to reveal a hole in the stone. Her breaths quickened.

"Pierce!"

He joined her as she clawed her way through the ivy.

"Well I'll be," he said with a laugh. "A cave."

She laughed too. "And a fine place to hide treasure."

∞∞∞

Once Ginny and Pierce had torn away enough foliage to gain access, they exchanged excited looks and ducked into the cave. Pierce took the lead and grabbed Ginny's hand as they moved into the dark abyss of the cave. The air inside was cool and damp, sending shivers down her spine as they ventured further into the unknown. The cave was narrow and low, forcing Pierce to remain stooped. The sound of their footsteps reverberated against the walls as they moved further in.

Ginny pulled on Pierce's hand. "Markings," she said in a whisper.

Pierce moved close to the etching in the cave wall, just able to make it out in the faint daylight from the entrance.

"A date. Sixteen..." She peered at it and shook her head. "I can't make out the rest."

"Could be around the date of the civil war."

Pierce couldn't bring himself to say it aloud for fear of cursing things. But they had to be thinking the same thing. Someone had carved the date after depositing treasure here. Anticipation danced in his gut.

They continued until the light from the entrance vanished.

"Pierce, it's so dark." She put a hand to his arm. "Be careful, please."

"I know." He cursed under his breath. "Everything useful

was with the horses."

"Perhaps we should find Youssef. The cave isn't going anywhere."

"No, I can't turn back now."

Pierce's determination echoed through the darkness as they pressed on. He suspected she didn't want to turn back any more than he did. She trusted him for some goddamn reason, and he couldn't deny relishing having that trust. So, she tightened her grip on his hand, and they pressed on into the unknown depths of the cave.

"Keep a hand to the wall," he told her. "It's slippery underfoot."

"So long as there are no sudden drops."

"I'm going to move very slowly," he assured her. "But it's a small cave. I have my suspicions there are no dramatic caverns here."

As they ventured deeper, the sound of dripping water could be heard in the distance. The rhythmic echoes reverberated off the walls, providing a strange comfort amidst the eerie silence.

Pierce stopped abruptly and her nose hit his shoulder. "Pierce?"

"We're at the end." He ran his hand across the slick, uneven surface in front of him. Definitely no way out.

"The end? Surely not?"

"I can't feel a way to move further." He released her hand when he kicked something on the ground. "Wait a moment."

He inched her back with a press to her shoulder and knelt down to feel a pile of sticks and something soft—wool perhaps. Whatever it was, it was intended to be the start of a campfire. He shoved a hand into his jacket and found the flint, able to get a spark off it on the third try.

A flicker of light sparked into being on the ground. It grew into a fist sized fire that gave off enough light to reveal the hollow in which they found themselves.

Ginny eyed the fire. "I didn't think you had anything useful."

"A flint but not much more." He said straightening.

"Someone has left firewood here." He motioned to the small pile on the floor. "Which means people have most certainly been here recently."

"Perhaps the treasure is buried," she suggested.

He scuffed his foot across the ground. "This is stone. Just a thin layer of dirt."

"Blast."

Pierce removed his hat, ran a hand through his hair and leaned back against the wall. He closed his eyes, any excitement long vanished, leaving behind the heavy weight of disappointment in his heart. He should have given up on the idea of this treasure long ago.

Ginny went to him and wrapped her arms about his waist. He jerked slightly in surprise then softened into the embrace, curving his hands around her. She leaned her cheek against his chest. The chill of the cave vanished.

"We will still find the treasure," she said determinedly. "Just because it's not here, doesn't mean we are done."

"Or someone else took it."

"It was meant to be a great fortune. We would know if someone had surely?"

"One would think, but most of the tales of the treasure are rumor and hearsay." He hefted out a breath. "We could be on a fool's errand."

Ginny moved back enough to look at him. "I rather imagine you have had moments like this before. Were all your previous artifacts and treasures found easily?"

"Not a one."

"Well, there you go. So what did you do when you reached a dead end?"

"Literally this time," he muttered.

"What did you do?"

"Looked at the information. Asked more questions." His jaw remained tight as he shook his head. "I don't have time for this, Ginny. My *family* doesn't have the time."

"Are things really so bad?"

He looked at her grimly. "I returned to find them on the brink of financial disaster. My siblings tried their best to manage things in my father's stead but none of them were taught what I was."

"You're the heir."

"Precisely."

"There must be something that can be done."

"A great influx of money is what is needed. The creditors are baying for their pound of flesh and though I've found a great many interesting things, none are worth anything more than a note in history." He tipped his head back against the wall. "I never should have left them."

"I've met your family and I very much doubt a single one of them resents you for living out your dream."

"It's cost them dearly."

"Not yet, it hasn't." Ginny curved a hand around his face. "We're not done yet, Pierce. We will find this treasure."

Somehow, he couldn't resist letting her determination light a spark inside of him once more. He gave her a soft smile and kissed her forehead. "Spoken like a true adventurer."

The way she gazed at him, Pierce knew he couldn't simply walk away from this pursuit, even if he desired to. She had a desperate need to complete this task, almost more than his own need for the monetary reward, and he wanted to see a woman as smart and as determined as Ginny get the acknowledgment she deserved.

Chapter Twenty

If only Ginny could stay holding him forever. Nothing felt quite so right as being in his embrace.

But they still had treasure to find, and she had a disheartened Pierce to encourage. Ginny eased her arm from about his waist and put her other hand to his face, holding him so he couldn't look away.

"We will find this treasure, Pierce," she vowed. "No matter what."

And they'd save his family. Even if it meant giving up the treasure to some collector who would hide it away in his grand house. As much as she loathed the idea, she couldn't let Pierce and his family suffer.

"I know. But we cannot continue on in this manner."

For a moment, she thought he meant in regards to each other. Comforting him, holding him, felt almost more intimate than kissing him. The man exuded strength and confidence yet at present he needed her.

It was all she'd ever wanted. To be useful, wanted, needed.

"If we don't find something soon, I'll have to think of something else," he continued.

"Something else?"

"Some other way of sorting the family's finances. A new investment perhaps." He shifted his hands to her upper arms, and she felt his grip tighten slightly, as though using her for support. "I have my suspicions few people will wish to support me in anything new, though. I don't exactly have a reputation for being a steadfast upstanding British citizen."

Ginny couldn't bear the image of Pierce groveling for money in front of someone who couldn't see the intelligence and determination this man had.

"We will find the treasure." She set both hands to his chest. "And soon. We just need to—" she had an idea of what she needed to do but she wasn't certain she could go through with it yet. "We'll research more. We'll spend every night reading and every day exploring."

He gave her a half-smile. "What would I have done if I hadn't discovered you?" He took her hand. "Come, let's see if we can catch up with Youseff."

They made their way slowly out of the cave after Pierce stomped out the fire and he kept hold of her hand, even as they headed out of the forest and across the fields. Nothing had ever felt so natural as her hand in his as though they fit perfectly together. While it made her feel slightly giddy and light-headed, it left her with a sense of certainty. No matter what, they would get through this together.

And that meant she owed Pierce the truth.

Ginny swallowed hard and focused on the feel of his firm hand around hers.

"You know," she said, voice trembling. "I'm actually in hiding from my fiancé."

He froze, bringing them both to a halt in the middle of the field. Slowly, he turned to face her. He stared at her for several painful heartbeats, brows furrowed.

"Fiancé?" he repeated.

"Yes," she said, feeling the odd smile tremble on her lips. "Decided I didn't fancy marrying such a horrible man and ran for it. Even stole his carriage." She let out a shaky laugh that sounded ridiculous to her ears.

Yet already she felt lighter. The secret didn't weigh on her chest or linger in her mind. Pierce had put a lot of faith in her without asking questions or demanding the truth from her, and he deserved better.

"Ginny—" he released her hand "—what the devil do you mean?"

Hands clasped in front of her, she stared at a bare patch in the grass just behind him. She didn't like the pained look in his eyes and the distinct sensation he felt betrayed by the truth.

"Well, it was to be an arranged marriage you see. His name is Sir Horace Robertson. He hails from Scotland, and we had never met and—"

"You agreed to an arranged marriage?"

"He's a historian—a rather famous one at that."

Pierce rubbed his brow with a finger. "Ah."

"I imagined I might be useful to him somehow. Aid in his research perhaps or at the very least, expand my knowledge through him. You hear of these wives or sisters who help these important men and, if they do not get credit, they at least get to learn new skills and be of use to the world." She clamped her lips together. "I'm rambling."

"No." He shook his head. "Well, you are, but do go on. Why did you decide against the arrangement?"

"Well, we finally met and" —Ginny took a deep breath and willed away the humiliation that heated her from head to toe— "he declared me rather too ugly to be his wife."

"So why did you run?"

"He didn't want to break the arrangement, however." She lifted a shoulder. "I'm not really certain why. So he decided I would be hidden away in Scotland. I would be his wife, raise his children, and never be seen again."

Ginny didn't mention the awful, forced kiss. It would only anger Pierce further.

Pierce curled a fist. "Like some sort of broodmare."

"Truth be told, it all feels a little dramatic, running away and disguising myself as a boy, but if you had been there, Pierce, if you had heard how he spoke to me...I just couldn't stand there and accept that as my fate." She kept her trembling hands laced tightly together. "I had no doubt in my mind he would not free me from the engagement and I would be forced to wed him.

Something in my—" She pressed a hand to her stomach.

"Gut," he finished for her.

"Yes. Something in my gut told me I was better off running so I did."

"You should always listen to your gut."

Ginny allowed her lips to curve. "Yes."

He scuffed his foot over the grass then met her gaze. "I'm glad you ran, sweeting. I'm glad you trusted your instincts."

"Even though I lied to you?"

"Believe me, I wanted to find out the truth many a time, but I trusted you had good reason. You're no fool, Ginny, and I'm grateful you trust me to tell me now."

"You're not angry?"

"Oh I am."

"Oh." She eyed the ground again.

"At him." Pierce pressed a finger to her chin. "At this Horace character. How dare he think he could lock you away? How dare he disrespect you in such a manner? If he was here—"

"Well, he's not." Ginny forced a tight smile. "And with any luck, he's back in Scotland, and as soon as this treasure is found, I will be free to be Ginny again."

A flicker of determination ignited in Pierce's eyes. "Then we shall find this treasure. We shall uncover it and reclaim your freedom together." He brought his hand to her cheek, his touch gentle yet firm. "I promise you, sweeting, that once we have the treasure in our hands, you'll have the freedom to do whatever you wish, and so long as there's breath in my body, I won't let that man anywhere near you."

Ginny felt a rush of gratitude for this man who had unknowingly become her savior. She had expected judgment and rejection when she revealed her secret, but instead, she found unwavering support.

∞ ∞ ∞

"So you just said goodnight and left her?" Youssef shoved a glass of amber liquor across the bar to Pierce.

Pierce took the glass and cradled it in one hand while he eyed his friend. Propped against the bar, Youssef was beginning to look rather at home at the Bluebell Inn. The taproom was quiet tonight and Pierce had heard mutterings of rain down south blocking the progress of coaches travelling north.

Pierce took a sip of what turned out to be brandy and mimicked his friend's posture, resting his elbows upon the wooden surface. "She said she was tired."

"We're all tired. It's been a damned long day. But that does not mean you just leave her."

"Well, what the hell else do you expect me to do?"

Youssef gave him a knowing look. What Youssef knew, and he did not though, he failed to comprehend.

They'd returned to the inn, Ginny was tired, so he walked her up to her bedroom and told her to get some rest. What else Youssef anticipated of him, he had no idea.

He took another sip of brandy and closed his eyes briefly, letting it warm through muscles that ached from the day's exertions then he turned to eye the quiet room. A few locals lingered around the fireplace and two old ladies played cards in the corner.

"She told me everything, you know," Pierce said finally.

Youssef straightened. "As in, why she's in disguise?"

Pierce nodded.

"And?"

"She's running from a fiancé."

Youssef issued a long breath. "Well, I did not expect that." He moved closer to Pierce. "How do you feel about that?"

"Like I want to hunt the man down and kill him with my bare hands."

"He hurt Ginny?"

"Not physically, but yes." Pierce tightened his grip on the glass of brandy. "And he threatened her."

"I'll join you in that hunt, I think."

"He wanted to marry her against her will and I'm guessing her family don't care enough about her to prevent that from happening." Pierce shook his head. "She reckons if she stays in hiding long enough, he'll give up on her."

"No wonder she ran." Youssef turned to face him. "But why did she tell you all this?"

It was hard to explain the day's occurrences to Youssef. Pierce wasn't quite certain what had happened either. All he knew was something had changed between them.

"She trusts me, I guess. And I promised to keep it a secret."

Youssef raised his own glass in a mock salute. "Well, old friend, I wouldn't advise hunting someone down in a state of drunken rage, but we certainly won't let her down."

"No," Pierce agreed. The last thing he would ever do is give Ginny up to some bastard who couldn't see the value of what he had in front of him. Why if he was this Sir Horace character, he'd—

"'Ere aren't you that adventurer chap?" A tall man with thin, sandy hair swayed toward the bar. "The Daredevil Duke?"

"Not a Duke," Pierce muttered then smiled genially. "That's me."

"I must buy you a drink." The man motioned to the barkeep then offered out a hand. "Tom Morris, purveyor of fine goods."

Pierce shook the man's hand and introduced Youssef. "No need for a drink, though," Pierce said, waving away the barkeep.

It looked as though Mr. Morris had imbibed enough this evening and Pierce didn't fancy anything more than the warm comfort of one drink tonight. His head was in enough of a state without the additional confusion extra alcohol would cause.

"So tell me," Mr. Morris said, "what's been your biggest find?"

"We've had a few," Pierce replied vaguely.

"But in terms of value." The man's brows waggled. "What's earned you the most?"

Pierce lifted his shoulders. "It's hard to say. The value of our finds tends to extend far beyond monetary worth."

"Well, you know, should you ever be interested in—"

Ginny's sister cut between Pierce and Mr. Morris, facing the man with her hands on her hips. "I do not think Lord Beneford is interested in your stolen goods, Mr. Morris."

"Stolen goods," the man spluttered. "I have no idea what you're talking about."

"I think it's time you went home, Mr. Morris," Maisie said gently. "Apollo can see you home if you'd like."

Mr. Morris swung a look toward the kitchen doorway, where the viscount lingered.

"Uh, no. I'll find my own way home." He nodded to Pierce. "Good talking to you. You can find me at the village store if—"

"Mr. Morris," Maisie prompted. "Time to go."

Mr. Morris held up his hands. "Fine. I'm going, I'm going." He slunk out of the building, muttering to himself about being an honest man just trying to do business.

"Never buy anything from the back of Mr. Morris's shop," Maisie warned. "He's not the most honest of men."

Pierce dipped his head. "Thanks for the warning."

"Why isn't Ginny with you?" she asked.

"She's tired," Youssef put in.

"Yes," Pierce agreed. "It's been a long day."

"You've been keeping her busy, Lord Beneford. I hope my sister's hard work will not go unnoticed."

"I fully intend to credit her, Miss Maisie," he assured her, "and her hard work has not gone unnoticed, I promise you. Without her help, I rather think we'd have failed before we even started and considering what she's gone through—"

Maisie held up a hand. "Wait. She told you why she's here?"

Pierce glanced about the quiet room. "She explained why she's in disguise, yes."

Maisie blinked a few times then a strange smile curved across her face. "Well, I'll be."

"What?"

"Ginny's always kept herself to herself. It took me long enough to get the truth from her, and, yet, she has told you everything."

Pierce glanced at Youssef who also smiled oddly. "Well, she trusts me."

"It seems she does." Maisie nodded slightly. "But here you are, drinking brandy."

"I'm not certain what you mean."

"I think you do, my lord." Maisie glanced over her shoulder at her fiancé. "I had better get going. Apollo won't wait for me forever."

"Why do I suspect that's not true?"

Maisie's smile grew as she bid Pierce and Youssef goodnight and returned to Apollo's side. Her fiancé kissed her, and a pang of envy struck Pierce when the man wrapped an arm around Maisie's shoulder, and she leaned into him.

"You want that too."

Pierce shot a look Youssef's way. "What?"

"You want that. With Ginny."

He opened his mouth and closed it.

"Something was different about you two today. You kept smiling oddly at each other. I knew then—"

"Knew what?"

"That you love each other." Youseff rolled his eyes. "For a clever man, you can be incredibly dense, and for some reason, that intelligent woman up there" –he thrust a thumb toward the ceiling— "doesn't seem to have much more sense."

"What's your point, Youssef?"

"How much more time are you going to waste pretending you do not love the woman?"

"Love?" Pierce's throat tightened as he uttered the word. "Love?" he repeated.

"Yes. Love. You might have heard of it. Exists between some married couples, tends to be prevalent in families." He motioned to the doorway where Apollo and Maisie had just left. "Those two are a fine example of it."

"Love," Pierce said again.

"If you take your chance, you could have something like that too."

"I didn't—" Pierce rubbed the back of his neck and tried to scramble through his racing thoughts. "I didn't know I was in love with her."

"Yes you did."

"Well, I'll be," he whispered to himself.

That would certainly explain why he couldn't cease thinking of her. After all, why would he not love her? He'd never met a better person. She was clever and kind and had more courage than anyone he knew.

"You love her, Pierce, so all that remains to decide, is what you're going to do about it."

Slowly, Pierce shoved away from the bar. "I guess there's only one thing I can do."

Youssef grinned. "Tell her you love her?"

He nodded. "Tell her I love her."

Chapter Twenty-One

T he light tap at the door made Ginny jolt.

"Coming," she trilled as lightly as she could, not bothering to retrieve anything to cover her chemise. Her sister had seen her in worse states.

She forced away the silly smile that kept refusing to budge. The last thing she needed right now was questions from her sister.

She yanked open the bedroom door. "Maisie, I—"

Pierce filled her vision. Nothing about him had changed since she'd seen him only minutes ago. His hair remained tousled, his clothing crumpled. The fragrance of smokey air clung to him.

Yet something about the way he looked at her made her shiver. Something about him was entirely different.

She stared at him for a few moments, her breaths turning raspy with anticipation. When he simply looked at her, his expression practically unreadable, she finally summoned some words.

"Did you...that is...is something the matter?"

He shook his head. "Yes."

Ginny frowned. "No? Yes?"

"There's something..." He wrung his gloves between his hands then gestured behind her. "May I come in?"

The formality of him asking to come into her modest room at the inn made her lips twitch. "Of course."

She stepped back and he entered the room, filling the space

and making her feel instantly warm, especially once he shut the door behind him. She wrapped her arms about herself, acutely aware of how thin the chemise she'd borrowed from Maisie was.

Taking a step back, she laced her hands together while he paced the short distance to one wall then back to the mirror, and finally stopped in front of her.

"Pierce, you are starting to worry me. Should I be worried?"

"Yes." He shook his head. "No."

"Pierce?"

"Maybe?"

"Pierce!"

His chest rose and fell as he audibly inhaled. "Fine. Here it is. I'm just going to say it because, if I do not, I fear I shall regret it forever, and perhaps you shall think I am the biggest fool in all of Christendom, but, frankly, I do not think I am. Loving you makes me the smartest man in the world."

Ginny blinked rapidly. She replayed the jumble of words in her mind. "L-loving me?" she spluttered.

Pierce's expression grew boyish, and she swore she spotted splashes of crimson on his cheeks, but it could have been a trick of the low lamplight.

"Well, yes."

"You" —she pointed at him— "love me?"

He nodded. "Rather a great deal it seems."

The words refused to sink in for a few heartbeats. Never in her wildest dreams did she think a man like Pierce would love someone like her. Yet, as she thought about it, it didn't seem so ridiculous. Old Ginny, the Ginny who had accepted the hand of a man she didn't know, would laugh at the idea.

New Ginny, the Ginny who had spent so much time at Pierce's side, struggled to find anything wrong with the idea. They worked together perfectly, and he encouraged her at every turn. He respected and valued her opinions, and he made her laugh every day.

And she loved him.

She laughed aloud. By God, she really did love him. It was

obvious to her now really.

A golden eyebrow lifted. "Ginny?"

"Forgive me." She pressed her lips together. "I just never expected...that is...well, I love you too."

Relief washed over Pierce's features, and his eyes crinkled in the corners. He reached out to take Ginny's hands in his, lacing his fingers through hers and drawing her close so he could press his forehead to hers.

"I couldn't stand another moment more of not saying it," he confessed.

"I didn't know," she said. "That is, I did know I loved you, but I didn't know too."

He chuckled. "I'm glad to have cleared things up."

"They're so, so clear to me now, Pierce. I love you."

He lifted his head and drew her into his hold, his hands settling at the base of her spine. "Then it's settled. We'll find the treasure, announce our engagement, and that bastard Horace won't dare to come near you again."

"I might even start wearing dresses again."

Pierce chuckled. "Wear that wretched ugly hat to our wedding for all I care."

"I'm rather looking forward to being a woman again."

"My woman."

She pursed her lips. "That's rather possessive, Pierce."

"Damned right."

Ginny laughed, throwing her head back slightly.

"Ginny," he said, his expression growing suddenly serious. "Can I kiss you?"

"What sort of a question is that?"

"A serious one."

She shook her head. This rakish man asking her permission for a kiss? She wasn't quite sure what she had done to deserve such happiness, but she wasn't going to let it go easily.

"Yes," she replied. "Yes, please kiss me or else I might go mad."

"Well, we cannot have that," he murmured before lowering

his lips to hers.

The kiss remained gentle, and she felt the restraint behind it. Unlike their previous kisses, that were rushed and unthinking, this was a kiss that spoke of promise. His lips moved against hers, eliciting a soft gasp from Ginny, her fingers curling into the fabric of his coat.

He moved away before she could deepen the kiss, his warm breaths drifting across her mouth and making her ache for more.

"I never want to let you go," Pierce whispered, his voice husky.

Ginny simply smiled, keeping her grip firm on his coat. "Then don't."

∞∞∞

Pierce hesitated. He should leave. He was only going to confess to being in love once in his life and he wanted to do it properly.

But, miracles of miracles, Ginny loved him. And he wasn't certain he could leave her side tonight.

He was certain, however, what would happen if he remained here.

And he rather suspected she did too. The damned woman would forever keep him on his toes. No one would have expected the fire lighting her eyes or the way her fingers moved from his coat to begin exploring the skin at the open neck of his shirt.

He held back a shiver at her touch.

Her smile was exquisite. She was exquisite. No one knew it apart from him and he loved that. Loved her. More than he ever thought possible.

That meant that as soon as she leaned in for another kiss, he couldn't deny her.

The flickering candlelight cast a warm glow across the room, its golden hues dancing on the walls of the cozy inn bedroom.

She'd changed into a thin chemise that drove his imagination wild.

Pierce couldn't tear his eyes away from Ginny's face, illuminated in the soft light. Her cheeks were flushed with desire, and her lips beckoned him closer. He leaned in, capturing her mouth in a lingering kiss, his hands cradling her face gently. Nothing else existed apart from her.

And those mischievous wandering hands.

She moved her hands to his coat and shoved it from his shoulders. He broke contact briefly to fling his jacket to the floor then took her face in his hands again. The kiss grew more frantic, more desperate. He wondered if he would ever get enough of the taste of her and concluded a lifetime might not be enough.

As their kisses grew more heated, Pierce couldn't resist returning the favor, tracing the outline of her waist and sliding his hands down to rest on her hips. His cock was as hard as a stone and the way she moved against him told him she knew full well what she was doing to him.

Who would have thought this bluestocking in disguise would turn into a wild temptress? He supposed he should have known from the moment he discovered her disguise. There was nothing plain or simple about this wickedly clever woman.

With a low growl, Pierce lifted Ginny and carried her toward the bed, laying her down gently. She grabbed impatiently at his shirt and drew him close. Her lips met his hungrily, her tongue darting out to meet his, sending waves of pleasure through his body.

He groaned, his hands tightening on her waist as he deepened the kiss, his tongue sliding into her mouth, mimicking the actions of his hands.

As their kiss continued to intensify, Pierce found himself losing all control, his mind clouded with overwhelming desire.

Pierce couldn't resist. He traced tender circles over her collarbone, down to her breasts, and finally cupped them, gently squeezing. She arched into his touch in a move so submissive, he almost lost control then and there.

Ginny moaned into his mouth, her hands gripping his shirt with an equal intensity. Then she broke the kiss, shifted and positioned herself on top of him.

Staring up at her, he struggled to believe this was happening. It was embarrassing to admit, he'd slipped into too many fantasies that looked just like this of late.

Her gaze locked onto his, revealing a beguiling combination of boldness and innocence, an echo of the traits that drew him to her so strongly.

Heart hammering in his throat, Pierce stayed silent, his unbelieving mind convinced that but one whisper would cause the vision in front of him to evaporate into the cold night air.

Her cool fingertips brushed across his jawline, rasping over his stubble, and trailing down his neck to his chest, wresting a growl from his throat. Finally able to summon the courage to move, he reached out hesitantly, his hand pressing against the delicate cloth of her chemise at her waist.

Pressing his thumb into her hip, he gripped firmly, holding her to him. A tumble of golden hair brushed against his chest as she leaned over him, teasing him with the softness.

Following the curve of her waist, he traced his fingers upwards until they brushed the underside of her breast and a sigh from her prompted him to cup at the delectable fullness, skimming a thumb over her hardened nipple.

"Ginny," he muttered before sitting up, hands sliding up her back to keep her firmly against him.

He pulled at the neckline of her chemise, continuing his ministrations while placing greedy kisses upon her collarbone.

Breathy sighs drew his head up and he found himself mesmerized by the motion of her mouth, her crimson lips parted in pleasure. He stroked his other hand up a soft thigh and he was rewarded with his name tumbling from her lips.

Ginny writhed against him, her body arching into his touch, her hips moving in a frenzy that matched the pounding of his heart. He'd never seen anything more erotic in his life. He had to taste her again, to feel her skin beneath his lips, his tongue exploring the sweetness of her mouth as he sought to discover every inch of her.

She gasped when the hand on her thigh pushed higher, and he skimmed the damp evidence of her desire.

He caressed every part of her and placed blistering kisses on her neck, her breasts. His tongue brushed her nipples through the fabric and moved upwards, pausing to taste the dip of her collarbone before nipping at her ear.

Moving his hand back up to the juncture of her thighs, he brushed against the delicate folds. Her face flushed and he kissed the blushes away with a smile. She stiffened as he rubbed his hand against her and slipped a finger inside.

"I will be gentle. Trust me," he whispered against her mouth.

"I do," she whispered back.

Chapter Twenty-Two

Ginny had put her life in this man's hands several times now, and now she was giving him control of her body. With gentle encouragement from him, she spread her legs wider and felt waves of pleasure coursing through her. She let out a gasp as he inserted another finger, the sensation both unfamiliar and delicious. Losing herself to the sensations, she moved against his hand and clutched at the sheets beneath her.

Ginny's entire body felt aflame as Pierce continued to explore every inch of her, his fingers moving with expert precision. She had never felt such pleasure before, and she found herself giving in completely to the sensations.

He continued to kiss and nip at her skin, driving her wild with desire. She wanted more, needed more from him.

"Pierce," she moaned, digging her nails into his back.

He trailed kisses down her stomach, making her tremble with anticipation. His hot breath on her core made her hips buck involuntarily and she let out a cry as he began to lick at her sensitive flesh.

She was lost in a world of pleasure and nothing else existed except for the feel of Pierce's tongue and fingers on her. She reached down to tangle her fingers in his hair, guiding him in his movements.

The tension within her grew higher and higher until finally she couldn't take it anymore. A wave of pleasure crashed over her, leaving her trembling, and panting beneath him.

Pierce moved up to kiss her deeply as she came down from

the high of orgasm, holding her tightly against him.

"I've never felt anything like that before," Ginny whispered against his lips.

"I'm glad I could introduce you to it," he replied with a satisfied smirk.

After a lingering kiss, he stood up and she immediately felt the absence of his warmth. As Pierce swiftly removed his clothing, she couldn't help but admire the sight of him naked in the soft glow of the lamp. He had been handsome before, but now he was truly magnificent. His masculinity was both intimidating and captivatingly beautiful. Unable to resist, she reached out to him again and he willingly came back down to her.

Pierce's body was lean and toned, the muscles defined and sculpted. Ginny couldn't take her eyes off him as he lowered himself back down to her, capturing her lips in a fiery kiss. His arousal pressed against her, and she couldn't help but moan into his mouth.

He touched the edge of her chemise, his fingers lightly brushing against her skin and causing goosebumps to rise. With a quick motion, he pulled it up and over her head. Ginny raised her arms to assist him in removing the flimsy garment, leaving her lying on the bed, bare and overwhelmed with excitement, unable to contain her trembling.

His touch was achingly gentle as he explored her skin, treating her as if she were fragile and his every move might break her. Unable to resist the sensation of his manhood brushing against her dampness, she eagerly moved to meet it.

Ginny met Pierce's fierce gaze as he positioned himself between her legs, their bodies aligning perfectly. With a deep breath, he slowly entered her, and they both let out a sigh of pleasure. He slipped in easily and she marveled at the unfamiliar sensation.

With one final push, he claimed her as his. Ginny bit her lip at the slight stretching sensation but as he began to move with more intensity, she relaxed into his touch and responded eagerly to each of his movements.

Who knew this could exist between a man and a woman? No one had taught her to expect such a thing and she suspected this was something special, something she would only ever find with Pierce. Ginny gasped her pleasure and wrapped her legs around him, urging him deeper inside of her. He obliged, moving in slow but steady thrusts that had her head spinning.

Her world narrowed down to the sensations of pleasure coursing through her body. With each thrust, Pierce drove her closer and closer to the edge, until she was teetering on the brink of ecstasy.

His hand found its way to hers and their fingers intertwined as they continued to move together in perfect rhythm. She could feel herself nearing the edge again and she held on tightly to his hand as she reached it.

With one final thrust, Pierce let out a primal growl and Ginny couldn't help but cry out his name. She clung to him as he rode out their release, reveling in the pleasure coursing through her.

As he collapsed beside her, pulling her close against his chest, Ginny knew that this was only the beginning.

"I never want this night to end," she whispered against his skin.

"It won't," he replied with a contented smile.

They lay there for what felt like hours, just holding each other, talking of what life might hold for them in the future, discussing their pasts and sharing sweet kisses. Ginny could scarcely believe what had happened, yet nothing ever felt so right and perfect.

Eventually exhaustion weighted her eyelids, and she gave into the warmth and comfort of his embrace and drifted off to sleep.

∞∞∞

When Pierce woke the next morning, he had to take a few moments to establish where he was. This was no tent in the desert, or a rundown inn tucked away in the countryside somewhere.

And, somehow, he was lucky enough to wake up to the most wonderful woman in the world. He couldn't help but smile as he remembered the events of the previous night.

Carefully, he shifted to look over at Ginny, sleeping peacefully, curled up in the tiniest ball possible against this side. Protectiveness surged through him, and he gently curled an arm about her.

She didn't need protecting, of course. He'd never met a more clever and determined woman. But that didn't mean he couldn't share life's burdens with her.

He should propose today, really. Of course, they'd spoken of marrying yesterday but it wasn't really a proposal. Ginny deserved a proper one. Perhaps his mother had a ring from some relative somewhere she could give him. They'd never really discussed him getting married and he suspected his mother was going to be shocked but incredibly happy.

After a few moments of watching her under the beams of morning sunlight that slipped through the curtains, he carefully extricated himself and slipped out of the bed.

Pierce washed his face and used a finger to scrub his teeth with the paste on the washstand. He caught the satisfied grin that clung to his face in the mirror and turned when he spotted movement in the reflection.

Ginny watched him with a soft smile on her face. "Good morning," she said and stretched.

Pierce turned to face her, his heart swelling at the sight of her tousled hair and sleepy smile. "Good morning," he replied, walking over to the bed, and slipping into the sheets next to her.

Her warm, soft body next to his made him clench his jaw. He refused to behave like a barbarian, but he couldn't deny he wanted to keep her in bed all day.

"Did you sleep well?"

"Surprisingly so," she said.

"Surprisingly?" He rather thought he'd done a good job of wearing her out.

"It's not every day I share a bed with a man," she reminded him.

Pierce wasn't prone to jealousy, however, a primal flare of pride shot through him that he had claimed this woman. He wouldn't tell Ginny that, however, for she'd likely scold him for being ridiculously old-fashioned and he'd have to agree with her. It didn't mean he didn't like the thought of having her all to himself, though.

He leaned in closer, brushing a strand of hair away from her face. "I can't believe how lucky I am to wake up next to you," he whispered.

Ginny's cheeks turned a light shade of pink, and she reached up to cup his face with her hand. "I feel the same way," she murmured before pulling him into a kiss.

Pierce wrapped his arms around her, pulling her closer as their lips moved together in perfect harmony. He had never felt this level of intimacy with anyone before, and it both excited and scared him at the same time.

When they finally broke apart for air, Pierce rested his forehead against hers, both of them breathing heavily.

"You know—" He paused when a heavy knock at the door sounded. He looked at Ginny. "Your sister?"

Ginny shook her head. "Unlikely."

The knock came again, and Ginny extricated her body from his hold, laughing at his expression when he finally released her. He gave her no quarter, watching her every movement as she quickly slung her chemise over her head, as if he could imprint the image of her smooth skin and petite breasts into his mind.

She inched open the door. "Youssef!"

"Is he here?" Pierce heard Youssef ask.

"Yes." She opened the door fully. "He's in a bit of a, well state of undress."

Youssef glanced between them as he stepped into the room

and Ginny shut the door behind them. "I hope this means there'll be no more pining."

"Pining?" Ginny asked.

"Oh, he's been pining," Youssef confided, and Pierce glared at his friend.

Youssef waved at hand at Pierce before he could say anything. "But unfortunately celebrating the fact you two will finally cease sending longing looks at each other must wait. You need to come home, Pierce."

Dread shot to his heart, making it pick up speed. "My father?"

Youssef's expression darkened. "Worse. Debt collectors."

"Damn it." He jumped out of bed and Youssef tossed the trousers he'd carelessly slung on the floor at him.

"I've got the horses," Youssef explained. "We need to return to the house quickly. They're threatening to haul away half the furnishings."

"Over my dead body," Pierce said through gritted teeth.

"I'll meet you downstairs." Youssef left and Ginny watched him dress, her arms wrapped about herself as she chewed on her bottom lip.

"Should I come too?"

"You stay here, sweeting," he said as he pulled on his shirt and ignored the laces. "I'll come back as soon as I've chased off the bloody vultures."

"Be careful," she said.

After chucking on his coat and boots, he took one more moment to curve a hand around the small of her back and pull her into him.

"Don't go anywhere," he ordered, lifting her chin with a finger. "We have a lot of unfinished business."

Mostly, he needed to propose.

"I'll wait here."

He kissed her firmly before he left. "Good girl. I'll see you very soon."

Chapter Twenty-Three

O nce Pierce left and she heard the creaking of the stairs, she moved to the window and watched him depart on horseback, his golden hair blowing in the wind. She spotted his hat on the nightstand and picked it up, smoothing her fingers over it as though she could somehow absorb some part of him.

It was hard to believe what happened last night. Hard to even comprehend what Pierce had confessed to her, yet she did not doubt his love for one moment. He left her feeling as desired and as treasured as the most beautiful young girl making her debut.

She only hoped he would return to her in one piece. Debt collectors were not usually the patient sort and were most likely the sorts of men who didn't mind throwing their fists around. If only there was something she could do but her family didn't have enough money to help even if her brother would part with it, and short of summoning the treasure from thin air, she could only offer her support to Pierce.

Well, she couldn't sit around in her chemise all day. She moved through her ablutions, tracing the tiny little marks Pierce had left on her skin and finding them oddly beautiful. She should probably help the cook with the morning meal. It would keep her occupied and this treasure business had meant she'd done little to repay Maisie's kindness.

After dressing and pinning her hair, she almost ignored the hat Pierce so hated. But the danger wasn't over. Not yet. The beautiful dream of a future with Pierce remained just that for now. Until she could ensure Horace was done with her, she wasn't certain she wanted to risk Pierce placing himself in some sort of danger to ensure her fiancé left her be.

She headed downstairs and into the taproom, already busy with customers. The front door opened, bringing with it a gust of wind and a few stray leaves.

Ginny's heart came to a stop. Maybe she had summoned him somehow. Maybe fate knew this had to be resolved. She swallowed hard when Sir Horace Robertson looked her way.

His gaze moved on swiftly and he marched over to the bar to speak with the barkeep.

Ginny eased out a breath but a part of her couldn't quite believe he hadn't spotted her. Her disguise was not that good. It seemed her face was that forgettable to him that he didn't recognize her even when staring into her eyes.

Nor could she believe he hadn't given her up. He could only be back to question Maisie of her whereabouts again, surely?

As he exchanged words with the barkeep, Ginny forced herself to take a deep breath. She had to be free of him once and for all.

Everything in her was screaming for her to run, to hide, to do anything to avoid being found out by him. But another part of her was defiant, refusing to let him control her any longer.

She remembered the excitement she'd felt upon hearing of his proposal. How she'd pictured life helping him with his research and learning even more of British history.

Horace finished his conversation and turned toward the door, ready to leave. This was her one chance, and she could not help but feel she had to seize it, no matter how terrified of him she was. Because not only could she ensure she was free to marry Pierce, but she might also be able to help him find the treasure as soon as possible and solve all of his family's money troubles.

It was a gamble. But for Pierce, she was willing to take it.

Ginny raced to the door and grabbed Horace's arm. He

rounded on her, snatched his sleeve from her grip and glared down at her. She watched his nostrils flare and caught the dismissive glint in his cold, steely eyes. She recalled that look when he'd first set eyes on her. She was nothing, no one of consequence. Her mind or her work ethic meant nothing to him because it wasn't wrapped up in a pretty bundle.

"I hear you're looking for Genievieve Beaufort."

"What's it to you, boy?"

A laugh almost escaped her. So forgettable was she, he hadn't even figured out her tones were decidedly female.

She pulled off her hat, taking a few grips with it and strands of hair dropped down her shoulders.

"What the devil?" he hissed. "You were here all along."

"Indeed."

"Damned conniving jezebels," he hissed, presumably referring to both her and Maisie.

She glanced around the busy room and nodded toward the private dining room. The last thing she wanted was to cause a scene in her sister's inn.

"Shall we?"

He gave a slight nod and followed her into the room. As soon as she shut the door, he turned to face her, his eyes burning with anger and betrayal.

"You," he spat, his voice low and dangerous, "are the most manipulative little hellcat I've ever had the misfortune to come across. How dare you hide from me? How dare you break our agreement?"

"The agreement was never for me to be hidden away somewhere like some shameful secret," she countered. "I was to be your wife, your helpmate." She lifted her chin, willing away the tremble in her voice. "I would have been a good wife."

"Did you really think a woman like you could be a true wife to a man like me? What would people think when they saw you on my arm? A successful, admired man with a plain woman like you," Horace scoffed. "It would be an embarrassment."

"You forced a kiss upon me!" she reminded him.

His cheeks stained a bright pink. "To see if you were really worth anything." He lifted his chin. "You were not."

"Then release me from this arrangement. You can claim you decided against it. I care little if I am ruined or not."

His lips twitched and his gaze skipped over her. "Do you really believe I still wish to marry you after this merry chase you have taken me on?" He laughed. "No, I knew once I found my carriage in such a state, without its wheels and looted of its luxuries, that I had a fine excuse to quit this agreement without a single iota of blame landing upon my shoulders."

"So I am free?"

"At least in terms of marrying me, yes." His smile grew menacing. "You did, however, steal from me, and the law does not look kindly upon the theft of vehicles."

Ginny's throat tightened. She opened her mouth to speak, but her tongue was tied. She felt a wave of fear wash over her as she realized that once again, she was in danger of losing everything she held dear. But there was no turning back now. She had to face the consequences of her actions and hope for a miracle.

"You're right," she finally managed to say in a trembling voice. "I did steal from you, and I am truly sorry. I didn't think it through, and I made a huge mistake. I will pay for the damage I caused, and I promise to make it right."

"You can make it right by facing up to what you did in the courts."

"And I will," she said, picturing Pierce and his family finally secure. "I'll even go peacefully."

His gaze narrowed. "Peacefully?"

"You can try to remove me from this inn, sir, but my family is known to these villagers and will surely intervene when they hear me screaming to the skies should you try to take me by force."

Horace's jaw worked. Finally, he gave a nod. "Fine. What is it you want before you will return to London to face justice?"

"Simply your knowledge, Sir Horace." She faced him head on

and drew in a deep breath. "I believe you might be able to help a friend of mine."

∞∞∞

They rode like the devil was on their tail to reach Pierce's family home to find his brothers in the doorway and a full-blown shouting match occurring between them and three men who didn't look any more clean cut than Pierce had hoped. He had no doubt these debt collectors would be eager to throw their fists around if they had the chance.

Pierce practically threw himself off his horse and Youssef took the reins without hesitation. Striding toward his brothers, he met Frederick's gaze and the tension eased from his brother's shoulders.

"Stop this nonsense at once!" Pierce thundered, causing everyone to turn towards him.

"Now, who the 'ell are you?" a man with a broad Somerset accent demanded.

The one next to him, as wide in the shoulders as the next but shorter than Pierce, rolled his eyes. "Another toff."

"Lord Pierce Elliot, Marquis of Beneford." Pierce stepped between his brothers and the three men. "And I'd like to come to an arrangement."

"The arrangement is," the short man said, "that we take your stuff and then your debts are cleared."

Pierce knew full well how this would go. They'd take some art and some valuables and those would be sold at auction and then the debt collectors would charge an exorbitant rate for their services and the debt would still not be paid off.

Pierce drew himself up to his full height, and smiled slightly when Youssef joined him. The man might be getting on in years, but he trusted no one in a fight more than Youssef.

"Actually I think you will find it's this." Pierce shoved a hand into his inner pocket. "You'll take this, for your services, and we won't knock your teeth out."

The accented man eyed the bank note Pierce offered out. "We're here to do a job."

"And you can do it. In a week's time if the debts are not yet repaid," Pierce said calmly. "But I don't like your chances against all of us and it would not be dishonest of you to say you could not gain access to the house."

Pierce could see the hesitation in the men's eyes. They were calculating their chances against Pierce and his two brothers. Youssef's imposing presence likely helped too.

The accented man took a step back, eyeing them all warily. "Fine. We'll give you a week."

Pierce nodded his head in satisfaction. "Good. Now get off our property before I change my mind about knocking your teeth out."

"We won't be so nice in a week," the man warned them. "And there'll be more of us."

Pierce folded his arms. "I'll have the money."

Once they were out of sight, Frederick turned to Pierce with a grin. "Well done, brother. You certainly know how to handle these types."

Pierce shrugged. "I learned from the best." He directed a thumb at Youssef. "Thank you for your help, Youssef."

Youssef simply nodded in response, his expression unreadable.

"Now," Pierce said, turning back to his brothers, "let's go inside and deal with this mess."

They made their way into the house and were greeted by their mother and sisters who had been anxiously waiting for them inside.

"Pierce!" His mother exclaimed, rushing over to embrace him. "Thank goodness you're all right!"

"We're fine," Pierce reassured her as he hugged his mother tightly. "Where's Father?"

"In his office. He's searching for letters about the debt. He's convinced he paid all payments on time."

Pierce drew back to see the lines of worry on his mother's face. "He's well today," she said softly, "and this has confused him greatly."

He eased away from his mother. "I'll speak to him."

Upon entering the office, it was evident that their father had been searching through papers and documents, trying to find the source of the problem. He looked up at them, his expression wearied.

"I don't understand," he muttered, his voice hoarse. "We've always paid our debts on time. We've never had any trouble before."

"All is well," Pierce said softly. At least it was for now. If he didn't find and sell this treasure soon, he had no doubt the men would be back and potentially with company now they knew Pierce was here to put up a fight.

Pierce's father sighed heavily and rubbed his temples. "I fear that isn't true, son," he said wearily. "From what I can gather we are drowning in a sea of financial troubles, though I do not understand why. Perhaps Mr. Green is no longer up to the task."

Pierce shook his head. The estate manager was doing what he could, but decisions made by his father in the early days of decline had already set the income of this ancient estate on the road to decline.

"I'll speak to Green," Pierce said, "and see what support I can offer. However, I do not believe he is doing a poor job. The issues we are facing...well, they are out of his hands."

His father pinched the bridge of his nose. "I cannot fathom it. We were doing just fine not so long ago."

"I'll take care of it, Father," Pierce vowed. "These current debts will be paid and there will be more than enough to ensure the estate continues to thrive."

His father narrowed his gaze. "How?"

He shifted on his feet. "Well, you recall Uncle Colin's lost treasure?"

"Oh, Lord, Pierce, do not tell me you have become obsessed with it too?"

"I'm close, Father, I know it."

"I was always willing to support your lifestyle. Being a duke is not the easiest and I considered that having a little freedom before you take up the title was no bad thing—"

"And I appreciate that—"

"But I cannot support you wasting your life on something that might not exist."

"I'm not wasting my life, I promise. I will find this treasure and all will be well again and I—well, I'll be settling down." Pierce traced a finger over a scratch in the desk before glancing up at the slow smile crossing his father's lips.

"Settling down? As in, marrying?"

"Indeed."

"To a fine woman I hope."

Unable to resist the grin carving across his face, Pierce nodded. "The finest."

"Well, I look forward to meeting her and having you around a little more." His father patted him on the back. "With a strong woman at your side, I have no doubt all will be well again." His expression grew sincere. "Even if you do not find this treasure, Pierce," he said. "We'll be well so long as we have each other."

"That's true." At least he still had days like this with his father and with any luck, he'd have more good days ahead of him where he could get to know Ginny and see how wonderful she was.

Chapter Twenty-Four

Arms folded, Horace glowered at Ginny from his seated position when she returned to the dining room with paper and a pencil.

"Can we hurry up? I have already wasted enough time chasing after you." He glanced her over, his lips curled in distaste. "And you could have changed into a dress. You look ridiculous."

"I was in rather a hurry when I left," she said calmly. "No chance to pack a dress, I'm afraid."

"Rather like dressing a sow in silk I suppose," he muttered as she sat opposite him and set out the paper and pencil.

Ginny ignored the jab. It didn't matter what Horace thought of her. He was a vile person with vile manners, and she was more than the sum of her looks which he would have discovered had he had the ability to see beneath them.

"Tell me all you know of Heversham Castle."

"Heversham Castle?"

"You must know it surely?"

He eyed her coldly. "Of course I know it. I just cannot fathom why you should have any interest in it."

"The sooner you tell me what I need to know, the sooner we can leave," she reminded him. "If my sister or her fiancé arrive, taking me to London will not be so easy."

He shifted in his seat and Ginny rather liked that he felt threatened by the idea of her family arriving. Apollo wasn't one for rules and she imagined Horace would be terrified of the man should they end up face to face.

"Heversham Castle," he mused. "Well, it was originally nothing more than a wooden fort but before it's destruction it was quite the luxurious castle."

Ginny remained silent. She knew all this already.

"Improved and expanded mostly to impress Queen Elizabeth," he continued. "But, of course, she only ever visited the once."

"What of its destruction during the civil war?" she asked, pencil poised over the paper.

"Well, it's position on the river meant it was of great importance to the royalists and that made it even more important to Cromwell."

Ginny tilted her head. "The river is some miles from the castle."

Horace peered at her down his nose, a slight smile tinging his lips. He took such pleasure in knowing more than her. She'd never been more certain that running from him was the best idea she'd ever had. Marriage to this arrogant beast of a man would have been a living nightmare. Even time in Newgate would be better than being married to him.

"It used to have a great mere." He gestured widely with his hands. "But Cromwell couldn't have such defenses survive lest the castle be retaken so he damned it up and drained it, cutting it off from the river."

"I thought it was just a moat."

He folded his arms and leaned back. "A common mistake. Lord Sutton painted it in the early eighteenth century and, from a certain angle, one could not see the river so every wretched fool since then forgot to make note of the fact, but it was indeed fed from the river."

"The river Duddon!"

"What?"

"Mary was talking about the Duddon River." She touched her palm to her forehead. "But of course."

"Who is Mary?" Horace's tone grew irritated.

"The river changed direction decades later in a storm," she whispered.

"Well, yes, but I do not see what—"

"Shut up." She held up a finger. "Just...shut up."

Whilst he spluttered to himself about how shockingly rude she was, Ginny wrote quickly, ignoring the gathering ache in her chest as she penned the words to Pierce.

"I know an awful lot more about the castle, you know. People pay me to give entire talks about a single castle. And here you are —"

She folded the letter with a flourish, wrote Pierce's name on the outside and waved it in Horace's face. "Do you wish to get out of here or not?"

She wouldn't admit it to Horace, but she didn't want Pierce returning before they left. It was time to face up to her rash actions and she wouldn't have Pierce winding up in trouble trying to defend her.

"Let us get a move on then." He ushered her out of the taproom, tutting as she handed over the letter to the barkeep before grabbing her arm in a pinching hold and hustling her out of the inn toward a waiting carriage.

"I knew your sister was lying you know," he said smugly. "I knew I had to return here." He shook his head and shoved her into the carriage. "I've had quite the escape from your rotten family."

Ginny settled onto the seat and rubbed away the sensation of his painful hold upon her arm, ignoring the annoyance flaring in her chest. A man like Horace was so convinced of his own superiority that there was no arguing with him. He wouldn't care that her sister was kind and loving and brave no more than he cared that she might have proved to be an excellent wife to a man of his stature.

"I do wonder," she said, after he'd instructed his driver that they were to return to London and sat next to her, "why it is you thought to marry me. After all, you are a man with a great reputation. I hardly think finding a wife would have been difficult for you."

He glanced at her and some flicker in his eyes suggested that, actually, yes, finding a wife had been hard for him. Perhaps too many women had seen beneath his facade to the bitter, arrogant man he was, or maybe the women of his choosing were aiming higher. A well-known intellectual was fine for many women, but not for those of rank who would be seeking at the very least a Baron.

"Your brother made it known you were looking for a husband."

But of course. She felt pity for her brother at times, who had made many mistakes in trying to lift their family into Society. Having the entire fate of his family on his shoulders couldn't be easy. But the damned man was prone to mistakes.

Offering her about on the marriage mart was most certainly one of them.

"I considered the fact your brother said you were a sweet, shy sort of a woman and that your sister will soon be Viscountess Chesham and decided I might as well take you on." He sighed and stared at the carriage wall opposite. "He never said you were so wretchedly plain." He finally looked at her. "Can you imagine me, a man of such renown, of such fame, admitting that all I could get for a wife was..." he motioned up and down with his hand "...you?"

Ginny rolled her eyes to herself. "I would have been a good wife to you, you know. I planned to be dutiful and dedicated and to quietly help you in every aspect of your life."

"Why on earth would I want your help?" he spluttered. "No, this is much better. Once you are convicted of theft, no one shall blame me for being indecisive or for breaking off the engagement. A man of my stature cannot be wed to a criminal, and I shall come away with my reputation entirely intact."

She understood now why he had been unwilling to let her go. He feared he would look weak perhaps, should he break off the engagement, or incapable of commitment even. And if she broke off the engagement, it would look even worse for him. All he cared for was his fame and reputation.

Propping her elbow against the window, she leaned on her hand and watched Oakfield slowly vanish, giving way to open fields and farmland. To think she'd considered Pierce to be no better.

She smiled to herself. She certainly knew better now.

$$\infty\infty\infty$$

Pierce and Youssef arrived back at the inn just as two carriage loads of people disembarked from their mud-strewn vehicle. Pierce flexed his hands on the reins while they waited for the carriages to move into the courtyard so he could stable his horse.

"Oh, come on," he muttered when one of the women waved at the front carriage to stop so she could retrieve something inside.

"Impatient to see someone?" Youssef said with a smirk.

"I'm going to ask her to marry me."

Youssef opened his mouth, closed it, and stared ahead.

Pierce suspected that was the first time he'd ever seen his friend speechless.

He patted his inner pocket to feel the shape of the ring box nestled reassuringly against his chest. All he needed was for these blasted people to get out of his way and then he could kiss Ginny senseless and propose properly.

Then they'd find the treasure, he'd make sure she got all the credit, and they could settle here in Oakfield with the occasional exciting trip across seas to keep that quick mind of hers busy.

He smiled to himself. He had it all planned out.

"Pierce!"

He turned to see Maisie shoving her way through the crowds of people entering the inn, followed by her brooding hulk of a fiancé. The man was tall and dark and about as refined in appearance as Pierce. All he knew of the man was that he was a quietly helpful sort of fellow and would do anything for Ginny's sister which meant Pierce wouldn't object to being his brother-in-law one bit.

The excitement threatening to burst from his chest vanished when he glanced into Maisie's eyes.

"Ginny," he whispered.

"She's gone," Maisie said as she reached his side, and handed him a note. "The barkeep said she was seen with a man who matches Sir Horace's description."

Pierce's heart slammed into his ribs. "Sir Horace? Her fiancé?"

"She went voluntarily by the sounds of it." Maisie nodded toward the letter. "Read it."

Pierce unfolded it and scanned the writing. Ginny would win no awards for penmanship, and he didn't like how hastily the letter was written.

"The river," he said. "Damn, she's only gone and figured it all out."

"The river?" Youssef leaned over from his horse. "What does that mean?"

"The treasure was taken by boat." Pierce shook his head. "But of course."

"Ginny said the river changed course decades ago," Youssef pointed out.

"So all we need to do is use the heading my uncle provided and see where it intersects with the old riverbed."

Youssef gasped. "The boat probably sunk."

"Indeed." He paused and re-read the end of the letter where Ginny reminded him of her love for him and explained her decision to accompany Sir Horace.

"But that doesn't matter now. Ginny isn't giving herself up to Sir Horace and any court of law while I have breath in my body."

"Court of law?" Youssef took the letter from Pierce. "Oh no. We're not letting that happen."

"They're heading to London, and they'll have to stop to change horses." He looked to Ginny's sister. "How long ago was she last seen?"

"About an hour ago." Maisie looked toward the courtyard. "We'll saddle up and follow you, but you should leave now. You could probably catch up with the barouche on horseback."

"Agreed."

"I'm going to fetch my pistols too." Apollo's jaw worked. "If this man thinks he can just take Ginny, he has another thing coming."

Pierce nodded and turned his horse. "I'll see you on the road hopefully."

He and Youssef came upon the first inn within the hour. Pierce knew it was unlikely Sir Horace and Ginny had already stopped but he wouldn't risk missing her. No one at the inn had seen either of them so they continued on.

Images of Ginny at the mercy of a man who had never once appreciated her rattled through his mind as they rode hard and in silence. He shouldn't have left her. He should have taken her with him and left her at the house where she would be safe until he'd scared this bloody man away.

When they arrived at the next stop, he didn't bother taking his horse into the courtyard, leaving it tethered at the front of the small inn and he strode into the low beamed tap room and straight to the bar. A young man greeted him with a nod.

"What will it be, sir?"

"Have you seen a man—" Pierce cursed under his breath. He didn't even know what the man looked like.

"Have you seen a man accompanied by a young boy?" Youssef asked. "A feminine looking sort of a boy?"

The barkeep thrust a thumb toward the room next to the taproom. "You probably mean the odd pair through there. Reckon it's a girl, though, with all that hair."

Pierce gritted his teeth as he followed the barkeep's gesture. He spared a brief moment to thank the man for the information then pushed open the door to the dining room beyond.

His gaze immediately fell to the figure sitting at a table in the corner. Ginny looked up, her eyes widening. Still in her boy's clothing, her hair was wild about her shoulders, and she looked pale and resigned. She shook her head tightly when he approached.

Sir Horace looked smug sitting opposite her. He seemed in no hurry to leave, devouring a pie and entirely oblivious to Pierce and Youssef's arrival. A serving girl stood nearby, a tray of refreshments held aloft, and she backed into the rear doorway.

"Sir Horace?" Pierce demanded.

"Oh, please, no questions right now." He wiped his mouth on a napkin and glanced up, his slight smile dropping swiftly. "Can I, uh, help you?"

"You can return Miss Beaufort to my care, is what you can do."

He looked at Ginny then Pierce and finally glanced at Youssef. "This woman is coming to London with me. She's a thief."

"She was a desperate woman, escaping an arrangement not of her making," Pierce said through a tight jaw.

"Pierce, please," Ginny said softly. "I'm willing to face the consequences of my actions."

"Like hell," Pierce muttered. He thrust a finger at Sir Horace. "She wouldn't have resorted to such measures had you not threatened her with being locked away like some sort of sinful secret."

Amusement flickered upon the man's lips, and he looked to Ginny then back to Pierce. "Well, this is rather priceless. Do not tell me you are interested in such a plain woman?"

Pierce slammed his fist against the table, making the plates and tumblers rattle. "I have more than an interest. I'm going to marry her."

Ginny gasped.

"And" —he straightened— "I demand satisfaction for such an insult against the woman I love." Pierce waved at Youssef who quickly picked up on what he wanted and handed over a glove. "A duel," Pierce said, setting the glove down on the table. "To the death."

Chapter Twenty-Five

"N o." The word issued from Ginny in a whisper. "You can't do this."

Pierce ignored her. As did Horace. The men eyed each other while the room filled with tension. People were seated around, silent, anticipating.

Breath held, Ginny watched Horace's throat bob and willed him to say no to the challenge. Pierce could die. Horace could die, and Pierce could be hanged for murder. Either scenario would leave her devastated. She'd only just found Pierce, she couldn't let him go now.

"Time and place," Horace said tightly.

"No," Ginny said again, and rose from the table and looked to Youssef who simply shrugged. She should have known her fiancé's ego would not allow him to say no.

"Now." Pierce nodded out of the window. "There's flat farmland over there. We can do it there."

Horace's tongue darted over his lips. "I have no second. Nor a weapon. Perhaps we should—"

"There you are!"

Ginny whirled to spy her sister marching into the room. The other guests at the inn watched Maisie stride over to the table, followed by Apollo who looked as though he might tear Horace limb from limb.

"What right do you have to take my sister?" Maisie jabbed a finger in Horace's face.

"She stole my carriage." He lifted his chin, but any bravado was swiftly failing now he was surrounded by so many people who cared for Ginny. She'd be enjoying it if it wasn't for the threat of a duel still hanging over them.

"I did agree to come with him," Ginny told her sister. "I came of my own free will."

"Precisely." Horace gave a firm nod. "She needs to pay for her crimes."

"Wedding a woman against her will is also considered a crime, Robertson," Pierce said, his jaw tight. "And I still demand satisfaction."

"Apollo, please tell him," Ginny begged her sister's fiancé. "There is no need."

"A duel?" Apollo's dark brows lifted and shrugged his large shoulders. "Seems like one way of solving this problem."

"Apollo," her sister hissed.

He leaned and muttered something to Maisie and though her sister's expression softened, disapproval still thinned her lips.

"I have pistols," Apollo said.

Ginny gasped. "Apollo!"

"We cannot duel now anyway." Horace's voice wobbled slightly. "I have no second."

"That can be solved." Pierce looked around the room. "Who here will play second to this man for fifty pounds?"

A gasp issued about the room and a young serving lad stepped forward. "Do I get paid even if I don't have to shoot?"

"Indeed." Pierce eyed Sir Horace. "And he will not have to shoot, will he?" He leaned closer to the table. "Because you're no coward, are you, Robertson?"

"Of course not." He rose slowly and straightened his waistcoat. "We'll need a doctor."

"You're all mad." Ginny looked at them all, finally falling upon Youssef's resigned expression. "Tell them, Youssef."

He held up his palms. "I would never get in the way of a matter of honor."

"Maisie?"

Her sister came to her side and pulled her close. "Do you really think Pierce will miss? Look, Horace's hands tremble already."

"But if he kills him…"

"I'm sure he will just clip him."

Ginny scanned her sister's expression. "I cannot believe you are condoning this."

"He took you, Ginny. He was willing to force you into a marriage you did not want." Maisie shrugged. "I'd shoot him myself for everything he said to you if I could."

"Find a doctor," Pierce instructed the boy, "and tell him we'll be out there, within the hour."

Ginny watched as Horace was guided out of the inn by Pierce and Apollo, followed closely by the serving lad. She could hardly believe what had just transpired. A duel? Over her? She couldn't let it happen.

"Youssef," she said, grabbing his arm before he followed them. "You must stop this. Please."

He gave her a sad smile. "I cannot. This is a matter of honor between two gentlemen."

"But if he kills him…" Ginny's voice trailed off, unable to even finish the thought.

"All will be well" Youssef patted her hand reassuringly.

"How can you be so calm about this?"

"I learned long ago that once Pierce sets his mind to something, no one can interfere," Youssef replied simply.

Ginny sighed and looked around at the remaining guests in the inn. Some seemed excited by the prospect of a duel, while others wore concerned expressions. Maisie stood beside her, brow creased with worry.

"Why don't you sit down?" her sister suggested. "We can wait here until it's over."

"Certainly not." If Pierce was going to risk his life for her, she was damned well going to remain at his side.

Once word of the doctor's arrival reached them, they headed out to the field. A small crowd had gathered, and Ginny's heart sank further into her toes. This would be no secret duel, able to be hidden from the authorities. If someone died here today, it wouldn't be kept a secret.

Pierce inspected the pistol, handed it back to Apollo and murmured something to Youssef before heading her way.

"Pierce, please—"

"I've not always done everything right, Ginny, but please let me do the honorable thing here."

"What if you're hurt?" Tears blurred her vision and her chin trembled. "All because of me. It's not worth it, Pierce."

He took her face in his hands. "You are more than worth it," he whispered as he gave her a kiss too light and too brief. "You're worth more than every damned treasure on earth."

"But—"

"The duel has been set now. You know I cannot withdraw. And neither can Sir Horace."

She looked at the man she'd run from and almost pitied him. His ego had gained the better of him and his trembling hands and graying skin gave away his fear of partaking in this duel. She had a suspicion everyone was right, and Pierce was the superior shot. An academic like Horace probably didn't spend much time shooting and he'd never been to war.

That still didn't make Ginny any more comfortable with this situation. Pierce's life was on the line and as awful as Horace was, she didn't wish death upon him.

Ginny watched as Pierce walked toward the designated spot for the duel, his steps steady and his shoulders squared. The crowd fell silent as they awaited the confrontation, tension thick in the air. She couldn't bear to see him hurt or worse, but she knew she couldn't stop this now. It was too late.

∞∞∞

Testing the weight of the pistol in his hand, Pierce spared Ginny a glance. Arms wrapped about herself, her mouth remained in a thin line, and he saw her shudder against the light breeze rippling through the grass.

He turned his attention to Robertson.

"You could kill him easily enough," Apollo said, his voice low.

A warning, Pierce reckoned. He didn't have any intention of killing the man, but a gunshot wound to the arm seemed an excellent punishment for everything he'd done to Ginny.

Of course, there was always a chance Robertson could die from his injuries. And that meant there was a chance Pierce could wind up in trouble, son of a duke or not.

It didn't matter.

He glanced at Ginny again and shook his head to himself. The damned woman was willing to give up her freedom, maybe even her life, so he could help his family. The image of rotting in Newgate had him tightening his grip on the pistol.

"Ten paces," Apollo announced.

By the time they'd taken their place, only Robertson, Youssef, Maisie, Apollo and the young boy remained. The crowd who had followed them out of the inn weren't foolish enough to want to witness an illegal duel. Only the boy seemed eager for it to be done, most likely because he'd be getting a fine pay day after this.

"Ready?" Apollo called out.

Pierce nodded, his gaze locked with Sir Horace's. He spotted the fear lurking in the man's eyes, beneath his veneer of false courage. It made Pierce's blood boil to think of how close this vile man had come to forcing Ginny into an unwanted marriage.

Pierce took a step forward, his boots sinking slightly into the soft earth beneath him. Each step felt heavy, weighted with the possibility of a future without Ginny.

He gritted his teeth. There was absolutely no way he was leaving her to live on this earth alone.

As he reached step nine, he kept his grip firm and sure.

He turned.

A feminine cry pierced his heart. The spot in which Sir Horace had been standing was nothing but grass. Pierce swiveled his gaze about, and fury flared through him.

Horace had Ginny in his hold, the pistol pressed into Ginny's side. He moved the pistol to point it at Apollo who balled his hands at his side, then he swung it upon Pierce before pressing it back against Ginny.

"You really think I'm going to let you shoot me? Over this woman?" Horace's voice trembled. "She's not worth it!" he spat. "I wish I had never been so kind as to offer for you." He pulled her tight against him and jabbed the pistol into her side, making her yelp. "You're not bloody well worth it."

Pierce's heart hammered against his chest as he watched Horace abuse Ginny once again. His fingers tightened around the grip of his pistol, but he knew he couldn't risk shooting the man while he held Ginny in his grasp. Pistols were hardly accurate, and he'd never shot this gun before.

Horace's words made Pierce's blood boil. How dare he speak of Ginny like she was some worthless object? She was worth more than any amount of money or power.

Taking a deep breath, Pierce stepped forward, his eyes never leaving Horace. "Release her," he commanded, his voice steady but firm. "I won't risk her life for this. You've made your point."

Sir Horace sneered. "Do you really think I'll let you walk away with her after you stole my fiancée from me?"

"You won't..." Ginny wriggled against his hold, making Pierce's throat tighten "...have a choice."

Pierce caught Ginny's gaze, so sure and steady. He hoped he communicated the same certainty in return. Between them, they could handle anything, including this egotistical madman.

"I told you..." Horace muttered as Ginny squirmed again, almost slipping out of his hold. "Keep still or I'll damn well shoot."

She stilled, but Horace was forced to reposition himself. It was their chance.

Ginny stomped down on Horace's foot at the same time as Pierce lunged forward. The man released her with a howl of pain and Pierce grabbed Horace's wrist, squeezing so hard that the pistol dropped from his hold, dropping harmlessly onto the grass.

Before Pierce could draw back his fist and put Horace down, Apollo hauled the man close by his cravat, making Horace's face redden as he lifted him from the ground.

"Using a woman as a shield, Robertson," Apollo spat. "That's a damned cowardly move."

"I..." Horace squirmed and clawed at the hold the huge man had upon him.

Apollo swung a look Pierce's way. "What do you want to do with him?"

Truthfully, he longed to take his fist to that smirking face until Horace would never forget what happened here today.

But Ginny threw herself into his side, tangling her arms about him and holding him as though she would never let go again. He glanced down at her, his anger dissipating swiftly.

"Let him go."

"What?" Apollo eyed him as though he was going mad.

"He tried to kill my sister," Maisie protested.

"Let him go," Pierce repeated firmly, glancing at Ginny who gave a little nod. "I expect you to crawl back to Scotland, never to be heard from again."

Horace looked to Pierce, then Apollo and Youssef, and back to Pierce. "I'm still owed a carriage."

Pierce almost laughed. The man did have some bollocks after all.

"You're lucky to walk away from this alive."

Apollo grunted. "Agreed."

"You forget the carriage, Sir Horace," Ginny said sweetly, "and these two lords shan't spread the story of your cowardice far and wide. How does that sound?"

Horace's jaw worked and he finally snatched his hat from the ground, set it upon his head, and glared at Ginny. "I wish I'd never set eyes upon you," he muttered then marched off back to the inn.

"I'm not," Ginny said, looking up at Pierce. "If it hadn't been for him, I would never have come here."

"And I'd never have fallen in love with you," Pierce agreed.

She smiled as he curved a hand over her cheek. "I will miss one thing about dressing as a boy."

"Oh?"

"The boots." She looked down at the sturdy boots she wore. "I couldn't have stomped on his foot like that if I were wearing my own boots."

Pierce chuckled, relieved that the danger was over, and they could finally begin their life together. "I have to admit, those boots certainly came in handy today," he said, tracing gentle circles on Ginny's cheek with his thumb. "But I'm still looking forward to getting you into a pretty gown." He let his thumb linger on lips that he'd kiss deeply if there wasn't a crowd that included her soon to be brother-in-law watching. "Perhaps you might get a special one for a special day soon?"

A crease appeared between her brows. "A special day?"

"A wedding, Ginny. To me."

Her eyes widened and a smile slowly crossed her lips. "Is that a proposal?"

"It's not my best use of words, I'll admit, but I'll be damned if I waste any more time not being engaged to you."

"We need to find the treasure first, but after that I do not see why we cannot wed."

She said it so matter-of-factly he almost missed that she'd agreed to marry him.

"So you'll marry me?"

"Yes," she said with a grin as she looped her arms about his shoulders. "I will most definitely marry you."

Epilogue

Shoving an errant piece of hair behind her ear, Ginny set her hands to her hips and eyed their progress. With the help of several strong men from the village, they'd dug a deep trench in what was once the riverbed leading from the castle.

Pierce came to her side, mud streaked and ridiculously handsome. She still couldn't quite believe she was soon to be his wife.

"Looks like we're making good progress," he said, his voice laced with excitement and anticipation.

Ginny nodded, her heart fluttering in her chest. They were so close to finding the treasure that had been hidden for centuries. It was a daunting task, but with Pierce by her side, she felt invincible.

"I wish my uncle was here. He'd have been thrilled to know his sketch meant something."

"Map," she corrected.

"I'd never have figured this out without you."

She gave him a slanted look. "I suspect you would have figured it out." He shook his head vigorously. "Eventually," she added.

Wind whipped across the grass, sending her hair curling across her face. Pierce pushed it behind her ear. "Did I ever tell you how delicious you are in trousers?"

"These fit a darned sight better than my old ones, to be certain, and I could hardly be digging in the dirt in a dress."

"Did I ever tell you how delicious you are covered in mud?" His voice grew low and wicked.

Tension coiled low in her body, and she gave his shoulder a light tap. "Stop trying to distract me."

"You distract me every moment of every day," he complained and put a hand to the back of his neck as he rolled his shoulders. "I don't suppose—"

Suddenly, one of the men shouted, pointing at the bottom of the trench.

Ginny and Pierce rushed over. The man slammed his shovel into something hard. "I think I found something."

Pierce scrabbled down and took the shovel from the man. Ginny followed him down, almost slipping on the mud in her eagerness. Pierce scraped away the soil with the shovel.

She forgot to breathe as he revealed a curved section of wood.

"A boat," Pierce murmured and dropped onto his haunches to smooth the dirt from their find with his bare hand. He turned to look up at her, his lips curving. "You were right, Ginny."

"It's a boat."

Any attempt at suppressing the giddy sensation welling inside her failed and she beamed back. They still didn't know if the treasure was in the hull, she reminded herself, but it didn't matter. They'd finally found something!

They wasted no time digging out as much of the hull as they could. Ginny watched on from the edge of the hole, her heart swelling with pride and love for the man in the mud-caked boots whose determination had brought them all here. They found more wooden sections, and slowly, the shape of the vessel began to emerge.

Pierce stopped digging suddenly and held up a hand. "Wait." He bent again and Ginny waited, heartbeat picking up speed, as Pierce carefully lifted something from the mud and held it up for all to see.

She squinted at the tiny object held between his fingers. "A coin?"

He grinned. "A coin." He smudged the mud from it with a finger and climbed up the side of the hole to come to her side and show it to her properly. "A coin with King Charles's face on it."

She took the coin and turned it over in her hands. "This is it, Pierce. You've found it!"

"No. We found it."

"I didn't just stand around," Youssef protested from the bottom of the hole. "Looks like there's more." Youssef's eyes widened. "Lots more."

Pierce chuckled and rolled his eyes. "I suppose we'll have to give him some credit too."

"I think that sounds wise," she agreed as he wrapped his hands about her waist.

She laughed when he pulled her tightly to him. "And you, Ginny Beaufort, shall be forever known as the woman who found one of the greatest treasure hordes in all of England."

"Which she found alongside her fiancé," she reminded him.

"And everyone will know about it, Ginny, I promise you that."

"All that matters is your family is looked after."

"I contacted the British Museum at Montagu House."

Ginny blinked a few times. "But why?"

"Well, I penned a letter a few weeks ago and I only just received a reply."

She frowned. "I don't understand."

"Should we find anything, they want to house it."

"But I thought you planned to sell the treasure to a private collector."

His grin turned so boyish she longed to kiss him.

"I know you were concerned it would be hidden away, but the good news is, the museum is getting too big and plans to rebuild it are underway which also means it shall no longer be by appointment only."

"But, Pierce—"

"And should this treasure be as valuable as we think, the museum is prepared to pay a decent sum for it."

Ginny opened her mouth to protest, but Pierce raised a hand, halting her words.

"I just thought you should hear everything before we decide what to do with it," he said with a soft smile. "We have a choice, Ginny. There is a chance a private buyer would pay more but by giving it to the museum we would be able to ensure everyone gets a chance to see this part of history."

She looked at the coin in his hand then back at Pierce. "Will it be enough?" she asked. "To ensure your family is well?"

"It will," he assured her. "So long as I take a bigger role in managing the estate's affairs. Considering I am settling down to be married to a rather wonderful woman, I should imagine life will consist of a few less adventures and more time to ensure my brothers and sisters are looked after."

"I rather hope there shall be some adventures still."

He pressed the coin into her hand and folded her fingers over it, then gave her a firm, deep kiss that left her breathless.

Drawing back, he held her face in his hands. "With you at my side, Ginny, I have no doubt there will be many, many more adventures."

THE END

Find more books by Samantha Holt on Amazon

If you loved this book, you'll adore this enemies to lovers story set in Oakfield when it first floods which can be read as a standalone. Meet Lilly and August as they are forced to join together to rescue the horse they're fighting over.
"Why do you have to be so infuriatingly charming sometimes?"
"Maybe because I'm not as heartless as you think I am."
"I never said you were heartless. Just aggravating."

Read on for Chapter One of Persuasions of an Earl's Daughter

Chapter One

She should have known he'd come.

The moment Lilly had received the news, she should have known.

And been prepared.

Instead, here she was, soaked to her skin, any remnants of curls long gone and plastered to her face and probably a little gray in color considering how cold the sudden torrent of rain had left her. She would not be so lucky as to look bright-eyed and rosy-cheeked after the sudden and short April shower.

And here he was all devastating and handsome.

The bastard.

Lilly plucked a damp strand of hair from her face and shoved it behind her ear. How had he missed the sudden torrent of rain whilst she had suffered its full onslaught? Typical. Though she was willing to wager, even wet, the man would still be handsome.

And devastating.

Lord August Beresford strode across the field toward her, his coat billowing behind him. Ivy clasped the reins of the horse and took a step closer to her as, though Spirit could hide her from him or at the very least offer some sort of shield. Inexplicably, her heart quickened its pace, echoing his efficient and easy stride.

Lilly supposed a man like the Marquis of Blackthorpe made many a pulse quicken. In fact, he probably had a multitude of physical effects on women. However, anyone who knew Lilly

Musgrave, knew men did not make her heartbeat quicken.

Until now it seemed.

She tried to swallow past a dry throat and ignore the way his gaze fixated upon her. Really, she should swiftly mount Spirit and ride off. She had no need for this confrontation and even less desire to stand sopping wet in front of a man the scandal sheets claimed to be the most handsome man in all of England.

Unfortunately, they were not wrong, and unfortunately her feet refused to cooperate with her desire to flee. After all, Lilly Musgrave never fled from anything. Her body and mind just simply did not know how to back down. Her competitive desire to win at all costs got her into a great many situations that could probably be avoided. Like this one right now.

The closer he got, the more she realized the silly caricatures in the newspapers had done him little justice. The early morning sunlight streamed about him, highlighting broad shoulders emphasized by a black, slightly faded greatcoat.

He was tall, something she didn't need to be close to realize. After all, her one guilty pleasure in life was the scandal sheets and August Beresford made an appearance in them on a regular basis. She couldn't deny there was something about how he'd been described that fascinated her. How must it be to be a man so blessed with wealth and good looks that one could simply breeze through life and do whatever one wished and go wherever one felt like?

He removed his hat as he neared. Lilly couldn't decide if her heart had picked up its pace so much that she simply could not differentiate between each beat, or if it ceased functioning all together.

"They lied," she murmured to herself.

She pressed her lips together and forced herself to take in a long breath whilst she planted her feet firmly, her grip on her horse's reins about the only thing preventing her from collapsing into a puddle.

August Beresford stopped a few paces from her.

The scandal sheets lied.

He was not the most handsome man in all of England.

His mouth curved in one corner as though something about her amused him. Golden sunlight glinted off his thick curls. A long, aristocratic nose led her gaze down to his chin, where a slight dimple sat as though God had decided the man needed at least one imperfection then got it entirely wrong, creating a point of utter fascination.

Her attention did not linger there long, though. How could it when he looked at her with those ridiculous blue eyes? No one should have eyes that blue, much less a man. And in any other face, they might almost look childish except when countered with the strong planes of his face it was nothing short of devastating.

He was most certainly not the most handsome man in all of England.

Lilly felt fairly confident in her assertion that he was probably the most handsome man in the whole world.

And all she had done so far was stare at him.

"No."

He blinked and the amusement switched to puzzlement, one tawny brow lifting.

"No?" he repeated.

It was all she could summon.

"No," she repeated.

No, she would not let herself be affected by something as superficial as good looks. No, she would not allow herself to stand here and gawp any longer. And no, she would not enter into negotiations with him.

There was one reason and one reason alone a man like August Beresford would seek a woman like her out.

He wanted something.

"Just no?"

Lilly nodded firmly. "You heard me."

"You have not even heard what I have to say yet."

"I do not need to. I know why you are here."

"My lady, I—"

"If you will excuse me, I should be returning home." She glanced him over as cooly as she could muster. "I'm sure your carriage is awaiting you somewhere." She peered past him to see if she could spot the vehicle on the road that wound past her father's estate. A man like Lord Blackthorpe probably took a carriage everywhere. After all, he would not be so foolish to let himself get caught in the rain.

"I desire but a moment of your time."

He said it so reasonably. As though he hadn't uttered a word that sent sparks through her mind. That would send sparks through any woman's mind.

Desire.

He'd know all about that word, she supposed. Too many women desired him. Why would they not? By all accounts, he was charming, adventurous, and worldly. Some even suggested he had a touch of the devil to him which for many a woman would only increase their interest.

She hated herself for feeling even the slightest inkling of curiosity or pretending she had some idea of what sort of a man he really was. She didn't know him. Devouring every sentence written about the man didn't mean anything. After all, words could be exaggerated. Made up even. She would do herself no favors by being fascinated by a man who only wanted one thing from her.

"No," she said one more time, managing to muster a little more volume. "No, you are not having my horse. Not today, not tomorrow, not ever."

∞∞∞∞

To say August Beresford wasn't used to women saying no to him was an understatement. Unless, of course, it was no, don't leave.

He smothered the amusement the thought caused him, knowing no wicked smiles would help him in this situation.

In fact, he wasn't certain what would. He wasn't certain at all what to do with Lady Lilly Musgrave. She was nothing like he expected her to be.

Approaching her alone had been deliberate. Manipulative even. He didn't want her young brother or father over her shoulder, watching their interaction closely. He certainly didn't want them trying to change her mind about selling the horse to him. It seemed, however, it was not a brother or father he needed to worry about. The woman had already made her mind up without a second's thought.

Glancing her over, August noted the lifted chin, the firmly set jaw, the hard gaze. He took in all of her in seconds. From the lack of a bonnet or hat to the dark, damp hair clinging to a long neck, down to a gown that might have been cream once but was hemmed with mud and plastered to a slender figure devoid of curves but intriguing nonetheless, most especially when one noted the twin points of her nipples poking through fabric not designed for a sudden shower. She should have looked vulnerable or at the very least unattractive.

But something in the way she held herself, in the proud rise of her shoulders and the shameless stance that said yes sir, I am cold, and these are my nipples, but I do not rightly care made her attractive indeed.

The attitude combined with wide dark eyes set against narrow features made him wonder if he should have done more research on Lilly Musgrave. All he knew of her was that she had been out of London Society since her family had fallen out of favor years ago and that the Musgraves were considered scandalous indeed.

How that was when the rest of the Musgrave daughters were all married off to men of good standing, he wasn't certain, but because of their self-exile to Bath and his years of travelling, he'd never come across any of them. He almost regretted it now. If he'd been a little better prepared, he wouldn't have a fight on his hands.

Or should he say a little tiff? He doubted she'd fight him

for long. She might seem unimpressed with him for now, but a few charming words and she'd be willing to offer more than her horse to him, he'd wager.

Not that he would take her up on the matter.

A shiver she tried to disguise with the bunching of her fists traipsed across her shoulders. Damn. He wanted her vulnerable to his deal, but he couldn't have her freezing to death.

"Perhaps this conversation would be better had if you were a little warmer." August took a step toward her and shucked off his coat.

Her brows knitted but she remained frozen until he slung his coat about her shoulders, and she flinched, and her eyes widened. It swallowed her and if it wasn't for the way her lips pulled into a grim line of determination, he might be guilty of thinking she looked rather endearing in his coat.

"Perhaps this conversation need not happen at all, Lord Blackthorpe."

"I only wish to make a proposal."

A hand to the lapel of his coat, she lifted it off one shoulder, paused, then released it, letting it drape back over her body. He'd half anticipated her throwing it into the mud, but it seemed he could not anticipate a single thing about Lady Lilly Musgrave.

"Well, I have no desire to hear your proposal, Lord Blackthorpe."

"A moment of your time is all I ask." He moved closer until they were barely a pace away from each other. He affected his best smile and waited for the harshness to leave her expression.

It remained. Hardened more even. His smile grew genuine, and she lifted her gaze to the skies with a sigh.

"A minute. Nothing more."

Before he could reply, she stuffed a hand under the coat and fished around before bringing out a gold pocket watch. August could only imagine where she had secreted it and his fingers twitched with the desire to feel the precious metal to see if it was warm from where it had touched her skin.

She flicked it open and nodded at him. "Go on then."

Damn it. She really did mean he only had a minute. "As you know, Icarus was my uncle's horse."

"I'm well aware of that." Lady Lilly's gaze remained on the clock.

"And you were gifted him in my uncle's will."

"I am aware of that too." Her tone insinuated utter boredom.

The slightest pang of panic struck him. He couldn't recall anyone ever seeming bored by him, even when he had nothing of note to say. In fact, he'd begun to take a slight perverse pleasure in muttering silly statements to see who was listening to him. Nine times out of ten, it went entirely unnoticed, and men and women alike agreed wholeheartedly with whatever ridiculous phrase he had just pronounced.

"I should be grateful indeed if you would consider selling me the horse."

"I—"

"I would pay more than he is worth—"

"How much more?"

"Ten per cent."

She smirked. "He is one of the best racing horses in the country."

"Very well, twenty per cent."

Lilly snapped the pocket watch shut. "No," she said simply. "And your time is up."

"No?"

"No."

"Are you not willing to negotiate?"

"I have no need of your money, Lord Blackthorpe, and your uncle willed me that horse because he knew I loved him greatly."

"He's a racehorse," August spluttered. "What on earth are you even going to do with him? He cannot live a sedentary life like your palfrey here."

"I am not ignorant, Lord Blackthorpe." She lifted a boot to the stirrups of the saddle and swung herself with ease over her horse. It was only then he realized she didn't even have a side saddle. Were it not for his coat covering most of her, he was certain he would see at the very least some bare thigh.

He wanted to see bare thigh.

He wanted to see more.

August forced his gaze to her face. A mere bit of leg wasn't going to distract him from his mission. He wanted that horse. Needed it even. And not just for the huge amounts of money it earned in flat races.

"You're no racer, my lady."

She flashed a grin. "That, Lord Blackthorpe, is where you are wrong."

She dug her heels into the horse and moved away with such speed it took him a moment to realize she was flying across the fields away from her home and he had no chance of catching up with her, even if he dashed back to the carriage awaiting him on the road.

It took him another minute for him to remember she wore his coat.

August shook his head and chuckled. Not only had he not negotiated the sale of his late-uncle's horse, but he had also lost a much-loved coat. It seemed Lilly Musgrave intended to put up quite the fight.

And a rather large part of him looked forward to the battle.

About The Author

Samantha Holt

USA TODAY Bestselling Author Samantha Holt is known for fun, witty, and usually steamy historical romances. She's been a full-time writer for longer than she ever thought possible having originally trained as a nurse and an archaeologist. She's a champion napper, owner of too many animals, mum to twins, and lives in a small village near the very middle of England.

She's usually writing (or napping) but when she's not, Samantha is plotting (books of course!) with her husband, drinking coffee, climbing hills that are far too high for her fitness levels or visiting stately homes and pretending she's posh.

You can claim a free book by signing up to her newsletter www.samanthaholtromance.com

Books By This Author

A Spinster For The Viscount

Some rebels deserve a second chance. Not this one, though...

Miss Maisie Beaufort has no intention of running away ever again. She's more than ready to return home after a decade in the midst of society and take charge of her life as a spinster businesswoman. Nothing will distract her. Especially not her first love, the rebel who destroyed her young heart...

Apollo Everly always knew Maisie was too good for small town life...and for a spare heir like him. He never stopped wanting her, though. Not that it matters. Even though he's reformed and a viscount, his lingering reputation is still a threat to her. He should stay away. But fate—and Mother Nature—seem to have other ideas...

If Maisie and Apollo want to rebuild their village after a devastating flood, they'll need to work together. The only question now is whether they can trust each other when it matters most. And if they can avoid heartbreak this time around...

Secrets Of A Duke's Daughter

A duke's daughter must be prepared for whatever life—and love —throws her way...

Lady Cassandra Fallon is finally ready to take control of her life and join her late mother's investigative society. She's more than confident she can do the job—even when her first case involves a potentially deadly scandal. What she's not quite prepared for is her brother's attractive (and increasingly distracting) friend acting as her self-appointed bodyguard...

When Lord Luke promised his best friend he'd keep an eye on Cassie, he meant it. But the brazen and entirely too alluring woman she's become is a far cry from the mischievous, freckled girl she used to be. Luke knows a lowly viscount has no business longing for (or touching) a duke's daughter. But against all reason...he does...

She craves independence. He only craves her. An epic battle of the sexes is at hand. But will love be enough to get them to happily ever after? Cassie and Luke will soon find out...

You're The Rogue That I Want

Red never shies away from a challenge.

Never.

But when Miss Hannah St. John strides into his life demanding —yes, demanding—he help her, he's certain she's more challenge than even he can handle. Hannah is determined to transport an artifact from France—one that will change everything—even if it means working with a lawless man like Red. Nothing is more important than preserving history. Nothing. Not even the touch of a smuggler who inconceivably makes her stomach twist.

When it becomes clear the irritating bluestocking will do anything for this blasted artifact and needs saving from herself, the earl-turned-smuggler steps in. Carting a cursed stone across the country with a know-it-all woman is not Red's idea of fun, particularly when their journey runs far from smoothly...so why does he find himself enjoying her company just a little too much?

Capturing The Bride

She'll do anything to escape her betrothed. Even if she has to plot her own kidnapping...

Grace Beaumont is desperate. Set to be forced into an arranged marriage to a depraved man, she's out of options. Calling on The Kidnap Club—an elusive group of men who specialize in helping women escape difficult situations—is her last resort. She never thought she'd end up hopelessly attracted to the rake who kidnaps her. And yet...she is...

Lord Nash Fitzroy doesn't get emotionally attached. To anyone. He especially doesn't get attached to the women he rescues. He's a protector, a defender, and an occasional shoulder to cry on. That's all. But the longer he spends in the quick-witted Grace's company, the more he finds himself struggling to maintain the professional distance he needs to do his job—and protect his heart...

She's in trouble. He's a rake with troubles of his own. They weren't looking for love. But what will Grace and Nash do when it finds them?

Printed in Great Britain
by Amazon